THE
FROM THE SEA

The prequel to *Children of the Shaman*

Jessica Rydill

MIDFORD
BOOKS

To Vicki Mihajlich with love

Kindle edition first published in 2019 by Midford Books
www.midfordbooks.co.uk

Copyright © 2019 Jessica Rydill

Cover design based an original photograph by Matheus Bertelli at
pexels.com

ISBN: 978-1-081-58902-8

The twins played amongst the rock pools, looking for crabs and occasionally stopping to splash each other. No-one else visited this cove, and they had it to themselves. The fishing port lay round the Cap to the east, tucked out of sight by the stony fishbone flank of a Calanque, grown from eroded limestone.

They were barefoot, having taken off their shoes and stockings and left them at the foot of the cliff, out of reach of the exploring tide. They had been coming here since they were tiny, and they knew the currents and the moods of the bay so well that they did not need to discuss them.

Aude swam in from the open sea. She paused some distance from the shore, treading water and watching the stranger children. Ever since her family moved to the village of Sankt Eglis a few weeks ago, she had been longing to explore this new landscape; in the forest where she had lived, pine cones fell and lay undisturbed for years, and bones would be found only after the winter snows melted.

Her older brothers had warned her against the dangers of swimming by herself, but Aude had ignored them. The sea called to her as if it was her natural element, one that had been waiting for her all her short life. She felt lighter than a spirit, bathed in fathoms of warm, blue water. Warm and clear; if she looked down she could see the seabed below her feet, though it was too deep for her to touch.

In her old home, the books she borrowed from the castle library described the adventures of long-dead seafarers, who set out to sail the world and its seven oceans: the Northmen who travelled many leagues in their ships called Drakkar with a carved dragon on the prow, until they found a new land further south, and sprang ashore to claim it.

This land known as Lefranu: home of the Franj, though in those days it was part of a forgotten empire. The Northmen had conquered a province, settled down, and become farmers and knights, lords and peasants; but some had travelled inland, further east, in search of new fiefdoms, land – and brides.

Aude had loved to listen to the stories told by her mother and the other women of the household. But those adventures had seemed impossibly remote when she was walled up behind stone ramparts, which themselves were guarded by trackless woodland full of green shadow and wild animals. A place where the leaves did not fall in autumn and the pines whispered together, echoing the voices of doves.

The waves held Aude like a warm hand. She had thrown off her clothes and left them on the beach, confident that this deserted place would be for her alone. Since her family moved into the Bastide, the fortified farmhouse her father had inherited from a distant relative, they had been busy scrubbing floors, brushing away cobwebs and killing spiders. There had been no chance to visit the local village, and her father and elder brothers had insisted that those were men's matters, in which the women of the family were superfluous.

Aude escaped at the first opportunity. She refused to think about her former home; too dangerous, those thoughts. At thirteen years old, she had been reborn into a new world in the South, where the sea was balmy, its salt bitter on her tongue, and the sky an arc of taut blue, a colour she could not name since there had been nothing so fierce, so burning, in the North.

The foreign children showed no sign of leaving. Aude splashed her hands in the water. Unknown currents could carry her out of her depth. She had learnt to swim with her friends in the river at home, where they were forbidden to go. She knew this was different; not bounded like a river, it stretched to the horizon, and its farther shore was invisible. Perhaps it carried on to the end of the world.

She could see them from here: a boy and a girl. They were sallow-skinned, with a tinge of gold from the early summer sun. She tried to work out what was odd about them. Unlike her, they were fully dressed, except for bare feet. Both wore black; the boy had black trews with a white shirt, the girl a black dress with white sleeves – an overdress with a chemise, perhaps. Though skinny, they looked strong and vigorous. They seemed to be infused with darkness, as if they had been steeped in vanilla pods, or locked away in a larder with cinnamon and cloves.

Aude decided to venture closer; she wanted to see how near she could go without them seeing her. If they noticed her, she would be gone in an instant. Something about them piqued her curiosity. Not just their appearance; they seemed to be playing in silence, except when one laughed out loud, or yelped as the other splashed them. She could not imagine playing with any of her brothers so comfortably; even the one nearest her in age was busy with 'men's matters', learning to hunt and ride a horse and wield weapons.

Aude slipped through the shining waves, whose flickers of watery light seemed to abet her. She was closer to the shore now, where the sea-bed shelved upwards. To her left rose a cliff, where white seabirds wheeled, taller than the castle's tallest tower. An eagle's eyrie, or the home of gulls; she wondered whether it would be possible to climb the wall of pitted, ragged stone, and the thought frightened her. Too high, too far, even when there were birds' eggs to be gathered.

She sank lower in the water, stalking her prey. She studied the boy and girl. He was darker than his sister, with inky black hair and smudges of eyes and brows. The girl's hair, the colour of oak, hung down in two stringy plaits. Her face reminded Aude of icons depicting the Mother: a dark face in the secret cavern of the chapel. It belonged in another world, where the saints and angels were stiff and enamelled; their hands raised in frozen benison and their heads surmounted with gold.

Aude blinked salt water from her eyes. The boy was laughing; he had a wide grin and a long nose. Without warning, and closer than she intended, Aude sneezed. And the children saw her.

Aude tried to hide under the surface. Only her head and shoulders should be visible, but the water was so translucent she feared the children would have a clear view of her naked form.

They looked frightened, like roe deer startled by an unwary huntsman; ready to run. They caught hold of each other, watching Aude as if she were uncanny. The boy shouted at her, but she could not understand what he was saying; he was not speaking Franj, or even the local dialect she found so hard to understand. He sounded angry.

Aude trod water, puzzled by their reaction. They must be used to encountering other people in the bay: bathers or fisherman. She pushed the wet hair out of her face, wondering who they were.

'My name is Aude,' she called. 'Aude d'Iforas. Who are you?'

The girl let go of her brother, and strayed to the edge of the beach.

'Are you a mermaid?' she said, shading her eyes against the light. Though she had an odd accent, she spoke perfect Franj. Aude laughed so much that she swallowed a throatful of water and sank. The girl gave a shout of alarm, and the boy dived into the water, fully clad, and swam to help her.

Aude did not want to be rescued, not with no clothes on. She tried to fight the boy off, but he seemed determined to bring her to shore.

'Let me go!' she shouted. 'I know how to swim. How dare you!'

The boy backed off, runnels of water pouring down his cheeks. Aude glared at him, tempted to slap him in the face. Something made her hesitate; she was a stranger, alone and a long way from help.

The girl waded into the sea, and said something to the boy in the language Aude did not understand.

'Who are you? What are you doing in our bay?' said the boy, ignoring his sister.

'What do you mean, *your* bay?' said Aude.

'Nobody comes here except us. The villagers never come. They say it's haunted.'

'I told you. My name's Aude. My family just moved to the village. My father has land here.'

The girl called again, insistently; she sounded cross. The boy turned his head, and shouted a reply.

'Are you foreigners?' said Aude.

The boy gave her a strange look. She was not sure what to make of it; he looked suspicious, fearful and angry all at once.

'We're Wanderers,' he said. 'The cursed people. That's why my family live on the headland. We're not allowed a house in the village.'

Aude stared at him. She knew the story of the Wanderers, cursed by the Mother for killing her Son; they were doomed to travel the earth until His return, though some, like Aude's own mother, whispered that it had been an unjust curse.

'Yudi, is she a mermaid?' shouted the girl. In Franj this time.

'I don't think so. I can't look, because she's naked.'

The girl on the shore screamed, and the boy shook his head.

'That's my sister. Our names are Yuda and Yuste Vasilyevich.'

'I don't think I can say those,' said Aude. 'How come you can swim?'

'*Mameh* taught us to swim when we were little. I've never met anyone who swam naked before. I'll lend you my shirt.'

'Yudi, what are you doing?' shouted his sister.

Aude watched the boy take off his shirt. She was reluctant to borrow it, but her clothes lay where she had left them, further along the shore. The boy thrust the shirt into her hand, and sneezed. On the beach, his sister was becoming crosser and crosser. Aude had to laugh.

'Thank you,' she said.

'You'd better put on my shirt before Yuste's head explodes.'

4

Aude pulled the sopping wet shirt over her head and wriggled into it. It seemed natural Yuda should take her hand and guide her to the sand, where his sister was waiting. Aude emerged, shivering in spite of the warmth, and hugging herself.

'Yudi, what have you done!' shouted Yuste. He pulled a face and replied without saying anything. Aude watched them, unaware that her mouth had dropped open. They were arguing in silence, waving their hands and screwing up their faces as if shouting at the tops of their voices. Aude touched Yuste's arm, and she flinched.

'How I can see you arguing when there's no sound?'

They glanced at each other.

'We can hear...' Yuste started.

'...each other's thoughts,' Yuda finished the sentence. 'We've got special powers. We were born like that. We can already do small stuff, like healing. When we come of age, we will be powerful.'

Aude screwed up her eyes, hoping she would not cry. She had known someone like that: a friend whose powers could not be mentioned for fear she might be burnt as a witch. They didn't even know what to call those magical abilities, the knowledge was so dangerous.

'You are...' she struggled to find a word. *Sorcerers, witches, magi*: those were the names for a forbidden skill, punishable by death in the place where she had grown up. But was the same true here? She did not know.

Yuste saw her distress. She touched Aude's arm. 'People call us *shamans*,' she said. 'They use the word because we travel into other worlds.'

Aude wanted to blow her nose, but thought it would be rude to use the sleeve of Yuda's shirt. Yuste must have noticed her sniffing, for she gave Aude her own, clean, pocket handkerchief.

'What worlds?' said Aude.

The twins glanced at each other. Yuda shrugged. Water was dripping off the coils of hair that framed his face.

'The underworld. Spirit worlds. Places beyond the mirror,' he said.

'Could you find someone lost?' said Aude. She did not want to say, or even think, her friend's name. That part of her life was dead; gone beyond recovery.

Yuda folded his arms across his chest. 'We can't do much.'

'Who was lost?' said Yuste.

'A friend. She disappeared.'

'I am sorry,' said Yuste. 'What did you say your name was? I didn't catch it.'

'Aude d'Iforas.'

'Are you a noble?' said Yuste. The prefix 'de' was the used by aristocrats and the gentry.

'It doesn't mean anything,' said Aude. 'My father isn't the Seigneur of this village. I don't think it has a Lord.'

'You must come from an odd place,' said Yuda. He was trying hard to avoid looking at her, as if he had remembered he was supposed to avert his eyes from a half-naked girl.

'From the far north,' said Aude, wishing he would meet her gaze. They had been close in the water, and he hadn't seemed shy of her then.

'I thought you came from the sea!' said Yuste, laughing.

'I've never seen the sea before,' said Aude. 'I think if I lived here, I would spend all my time swimming...'

'You have to be careful. There can be a current when the tide is going out, and you could be dragged under.'

'If you were born here... why do you speak that funny language?'

The twins exchanged a glance. Perhaps it had been rude to call it a 'funny language'.

'It's what our parents speak at home,' said Yuda. 'But we speak Franj as well. We were born here.'

'So you're not really Wanderers,' said Aude. 'You've grown up here, and this is your home.'

She meant it kindly, but she saw the change in their expressions. Their eyes became like stones; polished and black.

'We are true Wanderers,' said Yuda. 'We'll always be Wanderers. You're right this is our home; but the village is here,' he swung round, pointing inland, 'And our house is up there!' he pointed to the summit of the cliff, so high she could not see it.

'I am sorry,' said Aude. She sobbed, in spite of herself. Because she was uprooted, far from the only place she had known, with all the good days in the past. The one person she had loved gone for ever; and with her all hope, all prospect of the life Aude had imagined herself living, replaced with this new place, unfamiliar people, strangers.

'Where are your clothes?' said Yuste, taking her hand. 'You should get dressed. You look cold. And then Yudi can have his shirt back.'

Leaving her brother to mooch around on the shore, she followed Aude along the curve of the beach to the place where she had left her clothes. There was a small alcove in the cliff here, which was lower than the one where the twins' house stood. Yuste turned her back and stared out to sea while Aude used the alcove to change into her chemise, petticoat and dress. They were different to the fine clothes she had worn at home; made of homespun like the stuff peasants wore. Her dress was blue, and she wore an apron over the top to keep it clean.

She carried her shoes and stockings in one hand. When she emerged to join Yuste, the other girl turned to her with a smile.

'You mustn't mind Yuda,' she said. 'He gets a hard time for being a Wanderer. The bigger boys beat him. And he's not allowed to use his powers to fight back. You have such pretty hair. I've never seen true red before,' and she reached out to touch one of Aude's amber tresses, respectfully, as if it were something precious.

'It isn't a good colour,' said Aude. 'What do you mean, he isn't allowed to use his powers?'

Yuste glanced along the curve of the bay to her twin brother's distant figure; he was skimming stones over the water.

'Our powers can heal, but they can harm people as well. And as we grow, they will get stronger. We could injure someone.'

'If someone beat me, I'd want to hurt them,' said Aude. 'That's unfair.'

'I know,' said Yuste. 'Father made him promise never to do it. It could get us into terrible trouble. Wanderers have been killed for less in the past. And Yudi is so quick-tempered.' She spoke like an old woman, nodding to herself.

'I hope he does one day,' said Aude. 'It would serve them right. Then you and he could protect your family. Couldn't you!'

She made her hands into fists. The injustice of it angered her. Yuste stared at her with solemn eyes.

'I suppose we could,' she said. 'But father has worked so hard. He doesn't like violence.'

Aude held up Yuda's damp, crumpled shirt, which was drying fast in the sun. It felt as if she was holding his skin, or his shadow. The thought made her shiver and then laugh.

'What sort of magic can you do? I'd love to see some,' she said.

'It isn't magic. It's natural,' said Yuste, severely.

'What do you call it then?'

7

Their eyes met, and they laughed.

'Magic!'

They raced each other along the wet sand to where Yuda was standing, skimming stones over the sea. The shirt was drying on his thin back. Aude stopped and for a heartbeat thought she saw someone else there, a grown man, whose long black hair was caught by the sea wind. He turned to look at her, and she had the strangest feeling that he could see her, all the way through time, from his present to her past. But there were bloodstains on his shirt...

'No!' she shouted.

The figure on the shore turned round in surprise, and it was just the boy Yuda, with his short-cropped hair and pointed features. Aude felt her heart beating fast; she wondered what, or who, she had seen. She found Yuste and Yuda studying her with puzzled expressions.

'What's the matter?' said Yuste.

The wind was getting up, and it carried her words away. Aude ran towards her so fast they almost collided, and caught hold of her.

'I thought I saw a ghost!' she cried, breathless with running and fear.

Yuda joined her, and the three of them huddled together.

'You could join our gang,' he said. 'We have our own name, and a watchword, and a den on the beach. Or we could have a special one, just for the three of us.'

'Will you get into trouble for playing with Wanderers?' said Yuste.

'Probably. I'm always in trouble. It's my fault my family was banished!'

The twins stared at her. They looked alarmed, but also curious. Aude wondered whether they knew what banishment meant. Being Wanderers, they must understand exile.

'My family were expelled from the forest because...' She heard her voice tremble. Could she tell the truth, even to strangers? She was not sure what had happened herself. 'My best friend and I were trying to cast a spell, but something went wrong. She vanished, as if the ground had swallowed her up. When I told her father, the Seigneur, he refused to believe me. He thought she had been kidnapped by Wanderers, or killed. And he blamed me for her loss; he threatened to put me to the question. That's what they call torture. But my mother pleaded with him, and he was lenient; he could have had me executed.'

Yuste put her hand on Aude's sleeve, squeezing her wrist. 'How horrible,' she said. 'Was there nothing you could do to find her?'

Aude felt reluctant to face her. 'I don't understand what happened,' she said. 'She could make magic, same as you, and she asked me to help. We used to do everything together. Now I don't know where she is...'

'We'll find her,' said Yuda. 'One day. In a few years you'll be older, and you can help us search for her.'

Aude pulled a face. 'I expect my parents will marry me off,' she said. 'I'm already old enough to be betrothed.'

The twins gasped. Their expressions made her laugh in spite of herself.

'You're a *kind*, like us!' said Yuste.

'She means a child,' said Yuda, folding his arms. 'I hope they don't marry you off. I want to marry you!'

Yuste scolded him without saying anything out loud. He smiled and poked out his tongue. Aude knew Wanderers were not supposed to marry Doxans. And he was a small, runty boy whose spine bones stood out like a rack of potholders under his shirt. Her father wanted her to marry a noble, someone who had lands and wealth and status. He had an exalted idea of his social standing, when he had merely been seneschal of the castle; he was the steward, in charge of all the servants, including Aude herself as a lady-in-waiting.

'I don't want to marry!' she declared. 'I will become a nun. Then I can do gardening and lots of praying.'

The twins pulled the same face, as if they had each sucked on a lemon.

'I don't like nuns,' said Yuda. 'They drag you into church and try to convert you.'

'You're too young to get married,' said Yuste, sticking out her chin. 'We'll protect you. Look what we can do already!'

She swung round like a weathervane and pointed out to sea. Aude gazed along the line of her arm and saw a distant shimmer above the waves; out there the sky was dark and the water seemed to reflect it, as if a storm was hanging over the horizon. She shivered, wondering what Yuste was going to do. She could recognise the tingling in the air, like the atmosphere before a storm broke.

'Out there, under the waves, is a sunken city called Savorin,' said Yuda in a whisper. 'The fishermen say that at low tide you can see the spires of churches sticking out above the surface of the sea. And sometimes you can hear church bells...'

Aude shivered. 'What happened to the people?' she said.

He was gazing out over the sea, not looking at her. 'They drowned when the city sank beneath the waves,' he said. 'Their bones sit where they were when the water covered the place, surrounded by golden dishes and glittering gems. But no-one lives there now, except fish.'

'Did you really think I was a mermaid?' said Aude, trying to break the spell of the moment. He glanced at her; he was an odd, moody boy, as unlike her brothers as she could imagine.

'Could you be quiet, I'm trying to concentrate!' snapped Yuste.

'You're so slow,' muttered her brother. But he too sighted along the line of her arm with its pointing finger, and Aude saw, or though she saw, something like a blue spark, as bright as lightning, spring from Yuste's finger and shoot over the surface of the water, faster than an arrow. Just on the edge of vision, it hit the sea, and there was a fizzing sound and a puff of steam.

'What do you think?' Yuste said, turning towards them. When Aude was about to reply, she realised Yuste was speaking to her brother.

'I don't know what you were trying to hit,' he said.

Yuste scrunched her hand into a fist. 'I wanted to throw it as far as possible!' she shouted, red in the face. Yuda shrugged. 'It's not fair!' she said. 'I'm as good as you. I'm as smart as you, and I can run every bit as fast. Just because I'm a girl...'

Yuda looked down at his feet, scuffing the sand with his toes. Aude wondered what had upset Yuste. She could not understand what was going on, though she knew the frustration of arguing with brothers who believed they were superior because they were male. She wondered what Wanderers thought on this subject; she doubted they would be different.

'It isn't my fault,' Yuda said to his sister. 'We've always been the same. But girls are less powerful after puberty. You'll still be stronger than most people.'

'What does that mean, less powerful?' said Aude.

Yuda looked uncomfortable; small and crestfallen. 'Our teacher can already tell we're going to be powerful,' he said. 'At the moment, we're the same as each other. But when we're adults, I'm going to be stronger than Yuste. The way men have bigger muscles,' and he gave one of his skinny upper arms a forlorn squeeze.

'I don't want to grow up,' said Aude. 'I want to stay on the beach for ever, like this.'

'But if you did that, you'd be like those dead people under the sea in Savorin,' said Yuda. 'Frozen in the past.'

10

'Will the city rise from the waves one day?' said Aude.

'It's only a legend,' said Yuste. 'Mother told us that there isn't a city under the sea. Just rock formations.'

'There is a city,' said her brother. 'I can see it. You'd see it, if you knew how to look.'

'If we rowed out there in a boat, could we see it too?' said Aude.

'When Yuda says he can see it, he means only he can,' said Yuste, sullenly. 'You and I would probably see rocks, or seaweed.'

'Maybe he's making it up!' said Aude, who knew the ways of brothers. She wondered which one of them was the older twin; she suspected it was Yuste.

'I'm not making it up!' yelled Yuda, distraught that she doubted him.

Yuste shook her head. 'He isn't. He can really see other worlds. Spirit worlds. I can't do that yet. I'm better at healing. And I can throw my power farther. For now.'

'I would love to see Savorin,' said Aude, disappointed.

'We have gone looking for it,' said Yuda. 'We took our boat and moored it past the edge of the bay, close to the open sea. And we went swimming, diving even, to see if we could see anything. We couldn't.'

Aude gazed out to the horizon, where the shadow of a long wall of cloud seemed to hang suspended over the deep. It looked ominous; an incoming squall that would set the waves roaring against the rocks, and pounding on the sand as the tide came in.

'What is that?' she said, pointing.

'It looks like a storm out at sea,' said Yuste.

Yuda said nothing. He stared at the wall of cloud with his hands in his pockets, frowning.

'It's coming this way,' he said, under his breath, as if talking to himself.

'It can't be,' said Yuste. 'The wind isn't blowing from that quarter.'

He turned to her, and Aude saw the silent speech pass between them; they were so close that thoughts seem to travel between them instantly. She tried to imagine what that would be like; never alone, because there was someone who had always been there, a friend, since you were born. She could not help noticing that, in spite of their closeness, Yuda and Yuste were dissimilar, and not just in appearance; watching them argue in silence was funny, but also disturbing.

'...You shouldn't have done that!' said Yuda, erupting into spoken words. He grabbed his sister's arm by the wrist and pointed her hand out to sea, imitating the gesture she had used when firing into the bay.

Aude crept closer, and sighted along the line of Yuste's arm; out to where she had seen the shadow of the cloud, which seemed to be moving faster now she looked at it. And she saw something on the surface of the water, a shape that rode the incoming breakers like a vessel made from glass, so transparent she could barely distinguish it.

'There,' said Yuda. 'Do you see it now?'

'What is it, Yudi?'

Aude leaned closer to them, beginning to feel afraid. She could smell the change in the air, the coldness, like the scent of rain. The storm was coming inland.

Yuda looked from Yuste to her. Aude had never met anyone with such dark irises; from close to, they looked truly black. And she saw that he was scared; angry and frightened.

'Run,' he said. He caught Yuste by one hand, Aude by the other, and dragged them away from the edge of the water, heading inland. He moved so fast Aude was almost dragged off her feet; she had to twist and stagger round to keep up with him and his sister.

A sound was growing behind her; not the noise of a storm, but howling, as if all the winds in the world were rushing towards them, stirring up the sea and driving it after them. They ran headlong, and Aude, out of breath and disoriented, did not see how they could escape; the shorter cliff made a barrier between them and the land, and she could not remember how she had found her way down to the beach in the first place.

Between them, Yuste and Yuda dragged her to the foot of the cliff, and there were handholds, gaps in the rock, that she had to climb. Yuste went first, holding out her hand for Aude to follow, and Yuda came last, scrambling after her like a monkey or a sailor boy climbing the mainmast. Aude had learnt how to climb trees at home, but the cliff frightened her; only fear of what was rising from the deep kept her moving, finding handholds, until she fell face forwards onto a ledge, and found herself in a sea cave, a hollow amongst the rocks carpeted with sand and dry grass. She dragged herself into the centre, and the three of them crouched there, clinging to each other.

Aude imagined that if she listened carefully she might be able to hear the twins thinking. Yuda was panting fast, like a dog, and Yuste was trembling; Aude could not see what they saw, but she knew they were afraid, and that what frightened them must be fearsome.

The dark cloud was driving in from the sea, bringing long streamers of rain. The noise of the wind was deafening; Aude could see waves beating against the smooth shore where they had been standing, and engulfing it, until all that remained was a grey sackcloth of churning water. If they had lingered on the sand, they would have been swept away, dragged under by the incoming tide, and pounded to pieces against the rocks.

Yuda gripped one of her hands so hard it hurt, and Yuste held her other hand. Aude tried to yell against the noise of the wind and the sea, but she could not hear her own voice.

'Look down there,' said Yuda, pointing with his free hand.

They crawled on their hands and knees and lay face down, peeping over the edge of the cave. Out there on the waters, something glistened; Aude thought she glimpsed the shape of a boat, clear as glass, and someone standing up in the prow...

She shrank back.

'What is that? Who is that in the boat?'

The twins stared at her like owls.

'Yuste did it. She woke them from their sleep,' said Yuda.

'It's not my fault...' said Yuste.

Yuda snatched hold of their hands.

'We'd better stand up,' he said.

'Yuda, are you mad? If we stand up, they will see us!'

Aude did not hear his reply, but a second later he was struggling to his feet and dragging the two girls with him. The three of them clung together, staring down on the stormy sea; the water was grey and turbid, the colour of slate, and the glistening boat seemed to surge towards them, climbing.

In the prow was a hooded figure with a face of white bone and hollow eyes. It wore a silver crown. Aude could not tell whether it was a man or a woman. She could feel Yuda's body trembling, as if he were about to have a fit.

'Speak a blessing!' he shouted to his sister.

'I don't know what to say...'

The boat and the white-faced figure had risen to the level of the cave. Aude had a clear view of its skull face. She knew that if she looked into its eyes, she would go mad. She squeezed her lids shut, and hid her face against Yuda's shoulder.

'Please make it go away, Blessed Mother,' she said, praying to the one god she trusted.

Yuda spoke or chanted phrases in an unknown language. It was different to the speech the twins used to each other. Aude could not understand the words, but in her mind they appeared as fiery golden letters from an alphabet she had never seen before. Each of the letters was a flickering flame; they seemed to rise in the dusk between the three frightened children and the crowned figure in the boat.

Aude dared to open her eyes. Outside was a wall of dark grey, thrashing water, but something had risen between them and the onslaught of wind and waves: a thin veil of shimmering light, in which the golden letters were embroidered like threads onto a veil. From beyond it, she could hear the wind howling like an evil spirit, but it could not reach them; outside, the ghostly figure and the glassy boat dissolved back into the waves, which began to recede. As they disappeared, the lambent letters flickered and went out one by one, like extinguished candles.

'What did you do, Yudi?' said Yuste.

'I don't know. I spoke a blessing. One of the ones we say to keep us safe at night.' He shivered.

'I'm so sorry, Yudi. I never thought I would waken them.'

Aude saw him touch Yuste's face, and say nothing. She felt, and believed, that an indissoluble bond had been forged between the three of them. As if they had always known each other. It was odd to think how long she had lived in the forest, never dreaming about the sea, or imagining her path would cross those of any Wanderers.

Yuda kissed her on the mouth. It wasn't a child's kiss, but he seemed surprised and embarrassed by what he had done. Kissing a girl! That was awful. Aude touched her lips, feeling strange – shy and pleased. Yuste hit her brother, and laughed.

'Sorry,' said Yuda.

'You saved our lives!' said Aude.

He scuffed the sandy floor of the cave with his toes.

'Not just me. We all did it.'

'Did you see the golden letters?' said Aude.

The twins stared at her, unblinking, and nodded.

'But now I have woken it – what if it comes back?' said Yuste. 'What if it comes to our house in the night?'

'We'll watch out for it,' said her brother. He glanced at Aude. 'We're a proper gang now. The three of us. Like being blood brothers, or something. We're bound by a sacred oath. And our watchword is Savorin.'

The two girls repeated the word solemnly, and laughed at themselves. The storm and the turbid waters were draining away, slinking back into the bay and the emptiness of the open sea. The clouds had become normal storm clouds, cumulonimbus shrinking and losing their definition as the wind drove them inland.

'Don't tell anyone where you met us,' said Yuste. 'We try to keep this place secret.'

'I won't tell a soul,' said Aude. 'My parents would disapprove if they knew. And my brothers.'

The three of them stood at the edge of the cave and gazed out over the bay. The waves came in, broke and spilled slow froths of foam; the sea looked dull, a deep, silent blue that reflected the leaden sky. Far out on the horizon winked the light of a ship, or the beam of a lighthouse. Aude wondered which it was. It was riding at anchor, keeping watch over the deep waters where the city of Savorin slept with all its citizens, as if no-one had ever troubled their long sleep of death.

'I feel safe, knowing you are here,' she said.

'We're the Guardians of the bay,' said Yuda. 'And now you are too! Aude d'Iforas.'

***

When the twins arrived home, their mother was laying the table. Their father was in his study, which he used as a consulting room when he had patients, and their teacher was out the back, working the heavy lever of the pump to raise water from the well. With a hurried greeting to their mother, they ran outside, hoping she would not notice their damp clothes.

As they emerged from the house, Prakhash Sival looked up. He was a Darkman from Inde, with skin the colour of burnt sugar. The twins called him Teacher, or Guru-ji; though he was not a shaman, he was in charge of their training, and had been since they were small. He lived in their house, with his own room in the attic, and a few possessions. The twins loved him more than anyone in the world, and would have ignored their parents altogether, given a choice.

'Guru-ji!' they shouted, throwing their arms round his waist and clinging to him. It took Sival a while to disentangle himself. They were short for their age, though Yuste had started to put on height and weight.

'What is it, *kinder?*' he said, having managed to gently unwind their embrace.

'Did you see the...'

'The storm!'

They spoke rapidly; he knew they could still be frustrated by the slowness of speaking out loud. They often said the same thing at once, and gabbled; even now they were clutching at his sleeve with their thin hands. Something had scared them, and they were not easily scared; they had reverted to infancy, wanting to hide behind their mother or climb into their father's arms.

Sival hunkered down. He had learnt from experience how to win their trust; they trusted few people, except each other. They reminded him of shy wild animals that had not yet been tamed; a quality they shared with the shaman-children of Inde. He believed that, like horses, they were better trained with kindness, rather than broken.

'Tell me about the storm,' he said.

They stammered out the story, interrupting each other and repeating themselves; from time to time they would stop and argue using *sprechen*, their form of mind-speech. He could see how much it must have frustrated their parents when they needed to talk to them.

'There was a girl on the beach. Swimming in the sea...'

'A girl with red hair! She had no clothes on. I had to lend her my shirt.'

'She's new. We never met her before. She was swimming in the sea, in our bay...'

'We liked her. She wasn't like the others. She talked to us.'

'There was a storm and the dead people came from the sea...'

'Stop.' Sival held up his hand. They gazed down at him; solemn faces with round dark eyes. 'Did you say *dead people* came from the sea?'

Yuste and Yuda looked at each other. They might be sharing *sprechen*; he could not tell. Yuda folded his skinny arms across his chest.

'Yuste fired out to sea, and woke them. She didn't mean to do it.'

'I wanted to show her what I could do,' said Yuste, staring at her feet.

'The girl with red hair?' said Sival.

Yuste smiled into his eyes, nodding. 'She was so pretty! I wish I could have hair like that. And pale skin, with freckles. I've never met anyone like her before.'

Sival had heard of the arrival of the d'Iforas family; it was the talk of the village. The locals claimed they came from the far north, where people followed medieval customs and wore antique garb. Because the north had been isolated during the centuries of the Great Cold,

16

time had seemed to stand still. Though Sival would have liked to travel inland and visit those places, he knew it was too dangerous for a lone traveller. But he had heard of plans to build a railway north from the great sea port of Masalyar, the nearest city to Sankt Eglis.

'What did you think of her?' he asked.

'She was beautiful. I mean, really beautiful!' said Yuda.

'She was friendly, even when she learned we were Wanderers. And she seemed sad.'

'And the dead people from the sea?'

They nodded together, both solemn. Sival knew that, though they could be fanciful, and build wild imaginary games when they played amongst the rocks and coves, they could tell the difference between their imagined worlds and the other, spirit world that was beginning to open to them.

'Yuda says I woke them,' said Yuste.

'I knew the legend concerning a drowned city. But I believed... well, you read stories like that across the world. Stories about great floods, and sunken cities, and palaces where fish swim in and out of the empty rooms where once great kings held court...'

'They wanted to take us with them,' said Yuda.

'Don't tell your parents about this, *mes enfants*,' said Sival. 'They have enough to worry about. I will take the steam coach to the city and visit the library there. It may be that I will find something in the records about this legend.'

'Can we come too?' they both said with one voice.

'To Masalyar? You'd better ask your mother. But I can't look after you and visit the library.'

'We don't need looking after!' said Yuda.

'I would love to see the library,' said Yuste, with shining eyes.

Sival had noticed subtle differences between the twins. They had begun to appear when Yuste reached puberty. For now, her powers were stronger than Yuda's, but that would change once he reached puberty too. He worried about the disparity between the twins, who had always been so close. At home in Inde, this had never mattered, since all shamans practised non-violence and worked as healers – or magic-workers. They would only use their powers in self-defence, or to save others from harm. And though Inde was a traditional society, female shamans were treated as equals to the men.

Since Sival was the first emissary from Inde to Yevropa, and Yuste and Yuda his pupils, he had been making copious notes and sending long letters back to his homeland. Steamships and airships could travel that way, and he sometimes only had a few weeks to wait for a reply.

He knew there was going to be trouble. Though the family lived in this isolated rural community, far from others of their tribe, Reb Mordechai and Kaila observed the Law of the Wanderers; and the Law prescribed separate destinies for men and women. Yuste had to spend the days of her monthly bleeding secluded, and to take a ritual bath when it ended; her mother did the same. Meanwhile, Reb Mordechai was preparing Yuda for the time when he would become a man, and join the community of adult Wanderers; that meant a journey to the Beit in Masalyar, where he would recite a portion of the Law from one of the holy scrolls in front of the congregation.

This rite of passage was important, and Yuda was looking forward to it; but he felt the injustice to his sister, and so did she. Their parents had taught them how to read and write, and sent them to the village school when they were old enough; and Kaila had taught them to play the vyel, a small, bowed instrument. They had always treated the twins equally, and never denied Yuste an education – until now.

Yuste loved reading, and so did Yuda – except when he had to study with his father. He found it easy to learn Ebreu, the Wanderers' ancient language, because shamans picked up languages fast. But he loathed studying the holy books and commentaries with Reb Mordechai, who could not understand why his son found so little to interest him among their pages.

There was going to be trouble when Yuste and Yuda became adolescents, and changed into fully-fledged shamans. Shamans were unlike ordinary mortals; whether they were born male or female, there was a fluidity about their gender, and many of them would go on to desire both men and women. In societies where there were strict rules about marriage, this caused all kinds of problems.

Sival was sure his pupils would never be the kind of shamans who stayed within conventional paths, loving only the opposite sex as prescribed by religion and custom; they were strong-willed, rebellious and clever, and he had detected signs of their changeability, which was going to make living the strict life of devout Wanderers difficult.

'I wish we could read your mind, Guru-ji,' said Yuda. Yuste had rushed off to play without waiting for him.

Sival laughed in spite of himself. 'You have enough to worry about without reading the minds of the Teshvet, *meine kind*,' he said.

'Imagine what it would be like if you could overhear everyone's thoughts – mine, and your father and mother's, not just your sister's.'

Yuda sat down beside Sival on the grass. He was probably meant to be indoors studying. 'I suppose you'd go mad if you could hear everyone's thoughts,' he said. 'But it could be useful too. Like if there were bandits or Dzuzukim coming to attack the house and you could hear their thoughts in advance. And then we could fight them off.'

'You'd like to do that, Yuda? Fight them off?'

Yuda gave him a sidelong look, wiping his nose on his sleeve. He was still very much a small boy at times.

'I know you put a block on our powers, Teacher, but one day you'll have to take it off.'

'I'm afraid so,' said Sival. 'It happens when your power changes from blue-green to silver. I will notice the change in your durmats.'

'But *Mameh* and *Tateh* can't see our durmats, can they?'

Sival shook his head. 'I can see them because I've been trained to,' he said. 'But most of us ordinary folk, the Teshvet, can't tell you apart until you use your powers. That is useful too.'

Yuda looked up to the headland, where Yuste was running about yelling, her arms spread out like streamers in the wind. It was unusual for the twins not to be playing together, so Sival thought Yuda wanted to speak to him in private, something he had seldom done before.

'I'd like to be able to protect *Mameh* and *Tateh*,' he said, watching his sister. 'We don't often have problems with the villagers in Sankt Eglis, but from time to time you get troublemakers in the district. It's only because *Tateh* is a doctor that people have protected him in the past. And the Doxan priest is friendly...'

Sival smiled. He had met that worthy, an amiable, non-fanatical churchman, somewhat too fond of wine, who visited Reb Mordechai to discuss local matters. Though the family lived on the headland, this seclusion had partly been a choice of their father's, to protect them; living in the village they would have been too vulnerable to attack.

'So you would use your powers to fight,' he said. 'Not just for healing.'

Yuda glanced at him. 'Why not?' he said. 'It would only be in self-defence. And the bullies at school beat me up, because I'm small. And a Wanderer. I'd like to give them a surprise one day.'

'Your father has worked hard to maintain cordial relations with the villagers,' said Sival. 'There must be another way to deal with bullies. Other than violence.'

'I don't think so,' said Yuda, waving his hand dismissively, a gesture that reminded Sival of Kaila. 'They're too stupid. The only thing they respect is force. And *Tateh* always tells me the same thing, to ignore them and run away. He says we shouldn't get into fights with the Doxoi.'

'He's right,' said Sival. 'Your family are the only Wanderers in Sankt Eglis. Fighting with the local boys will get your family into trouble. You could all be driven out, and that would be a pity after your father's hard work setting up a practice here.'

'But if we lived in Masalyar, there would be other Wanderers for Yuste and me to play with. And we could go to the Beit every Kingsday. We could ride on trams, and you could go to the library every day. I don't know why *Tateh* decided to settle here.'

'He wanted to go somewhere where his skills as a physician were needed. And Kaila – your *Mameh* – thinks he knew that you and Yuste would be born different.'

Yuda leaned his chin on his hand. 'How could he know that?' he said.

'Where your father came from, in Sklava, shamans were not unheard of. And when your mother was carrying you, she believed she could hear you talking. In her womb.'

Yuda looked shocked. 'What did we say?' he said, staring at Sival with wide eyes. He had been a pretty child, but Sival could see that would disappear as he grew into adolescence. Perhaps it was just as well, as it would give the bigger boys less cause to beat him up.

Sival laughed, and shook his head. 'Kaila didn't tell me,' he said. 'She thought she was going mad, until she told your father, who confirmed that he had heard such stories in Ades, where he grew up. Both your parents were born in the Sklavan Empire, but they left and travelled to Masalyar, not long after the Thaw.'

He knew that Yuda had heard of his parents' emigration from Sklava, but loved to hear stories about their childhood there.

'Is he bothering you, Teacher?' said Yuste, suddenly standing over them. She could be jealous of Yuda's attention.

Sival shook his head. 'We were talking about the future,' he said. 'And what you will do when you attain your full powers.'

'Do you just wake up one morning and – bam?' said Yuda.

'It's more like what happens when your voice breaks. It doesn't happen all at once. And you have to learn how to manage your new strength.'

'Why does everything involve lots of work?' said Yuda, scratching his head under the skullcap he wore every day. His sister laughed at him.

'It's a pity you can't change places,' said Sival, and wished he had not spoken his thought so candidly. 'Yuste would probably prefer to study the Law, given half a chance.'

'She can study it, but she can't go to a yeshiva,' said Yuda. '*Tateh* wants me to go to a yeshiva and study to become a Rashim. And I can learn the Zahav and all the commentaries, and learn to argue about the meaning of the Law.'

Sival hesitated. He thought this plan unlikely to succeed. Not with any shaman, and certainly not with Yuda.

Yuste shrugged. 'It's useless being a girl,' she said. 'I can't do anything I want to. And I have to worry about modesty all the time. I don't want to wear long skirts. How can I climb the cliffs if I'm all trussed up in modest clothes?'

'If I go to Masalyar to study, you could come with me, disguised as a boy!' said Yuda.

Yuste looked shocked. 'I can't do that! What would happen when I...' she broke off and looked embarrassed; her cheeks turned red. 'I couldn't do it.'

'I believe there are academies for young ladies in Masalyar,' said Sival. 'Some may even admit Wanderers.'

Yuste shrugged. 'It's no use...'

The twins' mother emerged from the kitchen, her head wrapped in a turban, her sleeves rolled up, and an apron round her waist. She saw the children chatting with Sival and shook her head.

'Yudeleh! Yustka! You must give the Teacher some peace. Your father wants to speak to you both; he has an important piece of news.'

***

Aude ran all the way home; she knew her mother would be worried, and she risked a beating from her father, though he never hit her as hard as brothers. He might give her a few strokes of the switch on her hand or her leg; he had only beaten her hard on the day she returned alone, unable to explain what had become of the Seigneur's daughter.

The Bastide, with its stables and outbuildings built in the last century, seemed strangely naked and unprotected. Though the domain was surrounded by a high wall, the gates stood open all the time, and had rotted on their hinges. There was so much that was strange about her new life; people here had never heard of the forest, or the Seigneur;

21

and they thought the D'Iforas family quaint and outlandish, with their northern speech and their medieval clothing.

Aude's mother, Madame d'Iforas, had set to work making them all new clothes so that they should not appear too foreign and old-fashioned. At home, she would have spun and woven the cloth to make clothes as well, but to Aude's dismay, she went into the village and purchased some lengths of woven stuff from a pedlar, who had a supply of the worsted, linen and herringbone cloth that the local inhabitants preferred.

The men complained more than Aude and her mother, or the servants. They objected to wearing breeches or worse, trousers, since they were accustomed to putting on hose and long tunics that they wore over their shirts. It took some persuasion by Madame d'Iforas to convince them that people would think they were dressing like women in their rich cloaks and tunics. The finery of the court was reluctantly laid aside, and Gaudry and his sons complained that they looked no better than peasants or farmers, wearing shirts and waistcoats and corduroy or buff breeches.

After they had been dressed, Aude, her mother and her mother's women had spent a good time laughing and mocking the vanity of their menfolk. They found the country clothes easier to wear, move and work in than the long dresses, kirtle and hosen they had been obliged to wear at home. They had grown up knowing no other fashion, but they would not be returning there, and they were eager to dress the same as their neighbours.

Aude hurried into the kitchen, retying the strings of her white linen coif. Her mother and father were sitting at the large farm table, made for feasting apple pickers and grape harvesters, which suited their ideas of status. Aude curtseyed to her parents, and hurried to take her place at the board, where she sat below her three brothers, Claude, Thierry and Thibault, who was the nearest to her in age. Her mother had borne other children, who had died in infancy.

'Where have you been, child?' said Madame. 'You look as if you have been playing with the gypsies. Perhaps you are a changeling yourself!'

'Oh no, Maman!' cried Aude, who hated this joke of her mother's.

'I will say grace,' said her father, getting to his feet with a frown. As the head of the household, it was his responsibility to say grace before every meal, unless a priest happened to be visiting. The local priest seemed to find Seigneur d'Iforas intimidating; but as Aude had said to the twins, there were no seigneuries in the district, and the villagers were freemen and women, without the oversight of any bothersome nobles.

Aude pressed her palms together and closed her eyes while Gaudry invoked the blessing of the Mother and her Son on their repast. She had been chrismated and brought up a Doxan like her brothers, but Aude had a secret faith she did not mention to the men in her family; her mother had raised her to worship the Goddess, whose cult had long been celebrated in the forest.

The arrival of the Seigneur's ancestor and his men had driven worship of the Goddess underground, but the women at the castle followed Her in secret. Even the Seigneur's wife had been priestess of the Goddess; she went to chapel beside her husband and paid homage to the Mother and Son, but her women knew she was not a Doxan.

Nobody said anything in public; they knew that to stray from the true path would make them heretics, and the Seigneur would have them burnt at the stake. He was not fond of Wanderers either, or the tribes of Rom who sometimes made camp in the forest. In his own domain, he had absolute power of life and death over everyone, even his own family; and one day he had grown tired of his defiant wife, and decided to put her away – to send her to a nunnery.

Aude lowered her hands to her lap, and stole a glance at her mother. She knew Madame d'Iforas had sympathised with the Seigneur's wife, but no-one had dared to speak up for her, not even her children.

Aude's mother was called Aelis. Like most women at the castle, she came from a forest-dwelling family; the Seigneur's family and his retainers were descended from the Northmen, tall and broad, with fair or reddish hair, pale skin and bluer eyes. A few were dark-haired, but they all had those eerie, sky-coloured eyes; Aude's father was the same.

She was glad they had left the castle. If only the circumstances had been different! But she felt as if she had been released from prison.

The servants brought in the repast, and Gaudry carved the two capons that would be their evening meal. Aude wondered what sort of food the Wanderer children would eat. There had even been a Wanderer city just outside the boundaries of the Seigneur's land; she had been forbidden to go there, but she had seen the inhabitants in the distance, standing out in their black and white garments – a few even wore brown. She had tried to talk to those Wanderer children who strayed into the forest, but they were as shy as deer, and ran away at the sight of strangers.

The children of the travelling Rom were friendlier; they too worshipped the Goddess, though they kept it secret when they were passing through the Seigneur's domains. But they knew the girl-children from the castle shared their beliefs, and they would deign to play with them; even the boys were welcomed, though with more caution.

Not Aude's brothers, though. The older ones were lost to her; they were devout Doxans and well-advanced in their military training. The youngest boy, Thibaut, a square-set lout with tow-coloured hair, had taken special pleasure in tormenting Aude when he was younger. Now he tended to treat her with poorly disguised contempt. Like the others, he blamed her for their banishment from the castle.

Perhaps when the Seigneur banished Aude's family, he had believed it to be a harsh punishment, because the forest and the castle made up his whole world. For Gaudry, as his loyal seneschal, it had been an unjust punishment, when his daughter should have been the one to suffer; he blamed his wife for not teaching her better. Aelis herself seemed philosophical. She had comforted Aude and told her in private that they were better off out of the Seigneur's reach; there was a new world out there, where people no longer lived in the Middle Ages, but had clockwork engines and machines powered by steam and sparks of lightning.

Aude had seen little of the promised machines and other marvels yet; a steam coach came and went between Sankt Eglis and Masalyar once a week, but from what she had seen it was noisy and smelly, coughing black smoke from a tin chimney, and rattling and clanking like a giant kettle on wheels. It had not impressed her, but it did travel faster than a coach and horses; she would have liked to ride after it on her horse, but her parents had forbidden her to stray far from the village.

'There was a change in the weather this afternoon,' said Aude's mother, when the meal was finished and they were free to speak. Aelis dabbed her lips with a linen napkin. 'The sky darkened, and the wind rose. I thought there must have been a storm upon the sea. Did you see anything, Aude?'

'I did, Madame my mother,' said Aude. 'Something happened while I was walking down by the sea-shore. A storm rose up from the depths, and drove the waves inland. I might have drowned if it had not been for two children who rescued me. I think they are Wanderers.'

Her father threw his knife down on the table, and her brothers sat in silence and stared at Aude, who pretended to look at her lap in modesty, as a girl should.

'What!' said Gaudry. 'Is there no limit to your insolence, Miss? I have forbidden you to speak to the local peasants. And you say these were Wanderers? The accursed people, who Megalmayar drove out of Zyon after they killed her Son. You come of a noble lineage and should not speak to such people.'

'But My Lord Father, they were the ones who saved me! They were but children, and well-spoken. They used me with kindness and courtesy. And their father is the physician of Sankt Eglis. If they had not helped me, I would have drowned.'

'Better if you had drowned,' said Gaudry, folding his arms.

Aelis sat bolt upright and glared at her husband. 'My Lord, I cannot hear such wicked speech from you. And besides, I know you do not mean it. Thank the Mother that Aude was not washed out to sea! You should be grateful to the stranger children for rescuing her.'

Aude heard Thibaut snigger beside her. He might dislike her, but he loathed their father, who beat him because he was slow at learning and clumsy with weapons. He had reason to be glad that he would no longer be expected to train as a knight.

'Madame, you should not address me so in front of the children,' said Gaudry, turning redder. 'I forbid Aude to visit the sea again. She should not have strayed so far from the house without a chaperone. She might have been annoyed by some bold fellow who tried to take her maidenhead.'

'My Lord, you do talk nonsense,' said Aelis, shaking her head and straightening her wimple, which she continued to wear despite the fact she no longer needed an elaborate head-covering. 'Aude is a child, and we are far from the forest and its ways. She has but thirteen years, and is young to be betrothed. And she cannot have a maid or a serving woman following her about. You forget, my Lord, that we are no longer nobles, but farmers or gentry. You will make her look ridiculous, and myself also.'

'Where do these – Wanderers – live?' said Gaudry. 'Perhaps I should reward them in some way. It is not good to be in debt to such people. Perhaps their father will accept a purse of guineas. I have heard such folk are great misers and covetous of gold.'

Aude saw her mother shake her head. 'My Lord husband, you cannot give gold to a physician as if he were some peasant or merchant. The best gift would be something from your stores or your table. I think the best thing would be bread or ale, since there are certain foods forbidden to Wanderers. But a good, fresh-baked loaf is a suitable gift, and much better than gold. I myself will go with Aude to visit their house.'

'Woman, I forbid you! It is beneath your dignity and your birth to visit such places. And no doubt they live in a dirty hovel.'

'Nonetheless, I will go. If we are to live here, you cannot declare all our neighbours beneath my notice. Or how will I have gossips to share my bread with and help with sewing and women's work? You and our sons will be busy all day running the farm and supervising the labourers, when you are not riding out to the hunt or practising with your weapons. You are still a man of great affairs, Mon Seigneur, and this place has its own demesne and customs. It is a chateau in its own way, and you never thought to be master of a chateau, only the steward to a great lord.'

'Very well,' said Gaudry, his face creasing into a frown of discomfort at the sound of his wife's tirade. Aelis had learnt the art of talking her husband to a standstill, by being deferential and polite, flattering his vanity, and leaving him with the impression that she had followed his advice. Aude never ceased to admire her mother's dexterity. She knew it had been an arranged marriage, and her mother never seemed to be anything but a dutiful wife; the truth was very different.

Aude and Aelis were kept busy with work on the farm, where they too had to learn new skills; and it was nearly two weeks before they were able to visit the Vasilyevich house. It was a slow progress, because along the way, Aelis stopped to talk to anyone they met, and made no great show of being a noble or anyone's superior. What her thoughts were on the matter, she did not confide in Aude, but she was courteous and friendly when need required.

The local women appeared cautious, if not suspicious. In their eyes, Aude's family were foreigners from the distant and sinister north, who had no recent connection with Sankt Eglis, or the countryside near Masalyar. Gaudry's inheritance of the Bastide and its lands meant nothing to them, when he was an outsider.

And the countryside could scarcely have looked more different! Away from the cultivated fields, Aude saw golden, stony hillsides, barren except for a thick furze of thorns and wild herbs; the trees were stocky and sturdy, and her mother showed her the cork oaks that flourished in the dry landscape, as well as cypresses that stood up straight and black in the morning sun, and olive trees that grew in groves, dusted with silver leaves.

It was difficult to feel homesick when there was so much light, and the distant glitter of the waves (though Aude wondered about the hidden darkness of the undersea city; was it still there, waiting?) She was carrying a wicker basket covered with a cloth, and Aelis had placed in it the new-baked loaf of white bread, which they called manchet bread, instead of the black bread that peasants ate. Her mother had explained to her that this was a suitable gift for a physician and his wife, and would not smack of charity.

'You may be charitable to the poor, daughter, indeed it is your duty, but it is best not to flaunt your goodness. Everyone has their pride, however lowly their place in life. Your father has set himself high, being a noble, but here in the south we are no-one and nobody. I cannot tell him so, for it would make him exceeding wroth with me, and you too. But we are at best mere gentry, and must forget our pretensions. I think you and Thibaut will do better, since you are young; I doubt that my older sons will stay here, but will go to seek their fortunes somewhere else.'

It was a long walk to the physician's house on the headland, and though they set out soon after sunrise, by the time they reached the fields at the edge of the isolated house, the sun had risen high enough to make them sweat. Aude was wearing her coif, and Aelis had donned a broad-brimmed straw hat over her wimple – she wore one made from plain linen for comfort.

The two women stood still, staring up the incline to the odd house. It was different to the others in the district, the ones Aude had seen so far. In the village itself, the houses were roofed with red tiles, and their walls made from rubble stone, the same colour as the hillsides. This house had two storeys, and stood crookedly on the ground, its walls stuccoed and the roof made from a corrugated material – metal or wood, Aude could not be sure. All the windows had ornate wooden frames and shutters, and some had panes of glass, an expensive luxury bought from Masalyar.

The fields around the house revealed that the people who lived there grew their own food, not an uncommon sight in these parts. Though there were weekly markets in the nearby town, and the village had a communal bread oven, Aude doubted the Wanderer family used it. They had a scattering of olive trees, a fig growing beside the house, orange and lemon trees, and a walnut. Nearer to the house she could see the potager, where the family grew vegetables and herbs; chicken coops stood nearby, and chickens wandered amongst the fruit trees, pecking at the ground.

Aude noticed the brown man working on the field close to the house. He was darker-skinned than anyone she had ever met, brown as a horse chestnut, and clean-shaven. He wore gold-rimmed spectacles, and a long, pale blue shirt over some odd, pleated breeches. Aude watched him hewing at the stony ground with a hoe; she wondered if he was real or a spirit, a demon even, who the Wanderers had summoned to serve them.

'Look Maman,' she whispered. 'Who is that? He is darker than the Rom!'

'I suppose he must be a Darkman,' her mother said. 'Perhaps he is a Wanderer. Perhaps that is Monsieur Vasilyevich himself.'

They walked along the stony path that led between the orchards and fields, until they approached the potager where the Darkman was working. He became aware of their approach and put down his hoe, leaning on it; when they were nearer, he bowed and put his hands together in a gesture that must be some kind of salutation; it looked as if he was praying.

'*Namaste*,' he said. Aude did not recognise the word, and hoped it was not a curse.

'Good day, Monsieur,' said her mother, inclining her head with her best courtly demeanour. 'Are you the master of this house?'

The Darkman smiled, and now Aude could see his face properly, she thought it a friendly smile. He replied to her mother in perfect Franj, though with an unfamiliar accent.

'No, Madame. I am Prakhash Sival of Inde, tutor to the doctor's children. The doctor is not at home. May I take a message for him, or is it an urgent matter?'

'Is Madame his wife here, sir? I have brought a gift to thank her for her children's kindness in saving my Aude.'

'Is this Aude?' said Sival, smiling at her. 'The twins have talked about little else since that day. It seems the three of them had an adventure.'

'We did, sir, and they rescued me,' said Aude, breathlessly. She wondered whether the twins had told their teacher the truth; she did not want him to let her mother know what had really happened.

28

'So I understand,' said Sival. 'If you will walk along with me, Madame, I will bring you to the house. Please understand that Madame Vasilyevich is wary of strangers; she is not accustomed to being treated kindly by the Doxoi, though the villagers will now do much to defend their doctor. But as I have seen in my home country, times of fanaticism come and go, and old neighbours may suddenly turn on each other. It is a terrible thing.'

'Indeed it is, sir,' said Aelis, drawing Aude after her as if she were a much younger child. Not from wariness but because Aude was hanging back, feeling unexpectedly shy at the thought of meeting Yuste and Yuda again. 'We have seen such things in the north. In our old home, there was a town of Wanderers, which suffered from time to time.' She stopped, reluctant to mention that it was the Seigneur who had perpetrated these attacks.

They had reached the door of the house – the front door, at any rate, and Sival knocked on it, as if he were the visitor. After a pause, there was a rattling of chains and bolts, and the door opened on a short woman, with a pretty if sharp-nosed face, and brown eyes; her head was wrapped up in a turban of plain calico.

'What is it, Sival?' she snapped. 'Who are these women?'

Aude was shocked. She was used to customs of hospitality so strong that few visitors would be turned away without being offered water or wine, or a piece of bread. She thought the small woman looked at her crossly, as if she was an enemy.

'Madame Vasilyevich, this is Madame Gaudry d'Iforas and her daughter Aude. She has come to thank your children for rescuing Aude from the storm.'

Madame Vasilyevich dried her hands on her apron. She bowed rather stiffly to Aude's mother. 'You are very welcome, Madame,' she said. 'I am glad my children were able to be of service.'

As she was speaking, there was an eruption behind her, and the twins squeezed past, wriggling around her with the ease of monkeys, and fell out of the house to greet Aude, wrapping their arms round her – or Yuste did – and shouting with delight.

'Audie, Audie,' they cried, hugging her and laughing. Their excitement left the adults bemused.

'*Maman* made some bread for you,' said Aude, when they had released her. She uncovered her basket to reveal the loaf. 'We thought that bread should be safe, because it's clean.'

'It's beautiful,' said Yuste, staring at the bread. She threw her arms round Aude's neck. 'Thank you, thank you! No-one ever brings us gifts. They bring gifts for *Tateh* to thank him or to pay him for his work.'

'Goodness,' said Aude's mother. She looked at Madame Vasilyevich, and smiled. The small woman shook her head. 'Won't you come inside, Madame?' she said. 'Not many will enter a Wanderer house.'

'I should be delighted, Madame,' said Aelis.

Soon Aelis and Sival had been ushered indoors, leaving Aude alone with the twins; she had surrendered her basket of bread to her mother, though the twins seemed reluctant to let it out of their sight.

As soon as the adults were gone, they ran away from the house as fast as they could. They knew they would not have time to scramble down to the bay, so Yuda and Yuste offered to show her one of their dens on the crest of the headland, overlooking the sea.

The den had been made from the remains of an old sheep fold, left over from the time before the house was built. It was furnished with blocks of stone to act as seats, and filled with a muddle of toys and essential items: blankets, small bundles of firewood, pencils, which Aude had never seen before, a broken clock, a small spyglass for looking out to sea, and various lumps of stone, pebbles and shells.

'This is our den,' said Yuda, plonking himself down on one of the stone seats. 'The Vasilyevich den. That isn't our true name but *Tateh* had to adopt it after he left Sklava and moved to Lefranu. The officials at the city hall couldn't understand Wanderer names. *Tateh* should be called Mordechai Bar Yechiel, and my name is really Yehuda Bar Mordechai.'

'And I'm Yehudit Bat Mordechai,' said Yuste.

'Those names are too long, and difficult to say properly,' said Aude. 'But my full name is Aude Alazais D'Iforas. I have other names, from being chrismated, but I can't remember them.'

'Do they put actual oil on you when you're chrismated?' said Yuste, looking awed.

Aude nodded. 'Special sacred oil,' she said. 'But I don't remember because I was a baby at the time. The priest draws the wheel on your forehead and says prayers. It's very holy.'

'Wanderers don't do that,' said Yuda. 'Boys are *Brit milah*, and girls are given a name at the Beit.'

'What are those?' said Aude. The twins looked at each other. Aude guessed they were sharing thoughts.

'The Beit is our house of prayer,' said Yuste. 'There are several in Masalyar, where most of the other Wanderers live. Girls are given a name in front of the congregation. And boys are circumcised. It means...'

'The Rashim comes to your house and cuts a small piece off your... thingy,' said Yuda. The word made him laugh, and Yuste joined in. 'They cut off your foreskin,' he said, when he could stop laughing.

Aude clamped her hand over her mouth. She was shocked, but fascinated. No-one had ever cut off any part of her brothers, and she thought it might have improved them.

'How awful!' she said. 'Does it hurt?'

'I don't remember,' said Yuda. 'I was only eight days old when it happened. It's not always good because it's easy to tell you're a Wanderer. When I started at the local school, some of the boys took off my trousers to have a look. Luckily they don't do that any more. I didn't like it.'

'If they did that to me, I would kill them!' said Aude, making a fist.

The twins stared at her owlishly. 'But you're a girl,' said Yuda. 'And anyway... that's the trouble. I probably could kill them. Because I'm a *kind*, my powers are unpredictable.'

Yuste nodded. 'Your powers grow as you get older. But they change all the time, so you might singe someone one day and burn them alive by mistake the next.'

'There are people I'd like to burn,' said Aude.

They gazed at her, not understanding; Yuste patted her arm. Aude managed to smile at her. 'Are all Wanderers shamans, then?' she said.

Yuste and Yuda shook their heads. 'Most Wanderers are Teshvet, like everyone else. Our parents are too. That's why the Masters in Inde sent Sival to Lefranu. Shamans have started being born here since the end of the Great Cold. Sival is going to found a school in Masalyar one day. He is famous in Masalyar; they call him the emissary from Inde. And he can levitate!'

Yuste explained. 'When he meditates, he floats an inch above the floor. And he's not even a shaman!'

'I'd love to see that,' said Aude. 'I hope father will let us come here again. He forbade mother to come, but she never takes any notice.'

The three of them gazed down the slope towards the house. It looked to Aude like the witch's cottages she had seen in books of fairy tales. She wondered what was different about it: not the lime-washed plaster or the weathered stones of the roof, or the chimney stack.

'You house looks – odd,' she said.

'*Tateh* built it,' said Yuste. 'When he and *Mameh* moved here, before we were born. It's built of wood, with plaster over the top. And the windows have carved frames. *Tateh* came from a shtetl – a Wanderer village - near Ades, so he built a house like the one he grew up in.'

'It looks as though it's growing out of the earth,' said Aude. 'Or sinking into it. And I feel it's watching me.'

Yuda grabbed her wrist. 'Our bedroom is on the top floor,' he said. 'We have one room, *Mameh* and *Tateh* have another and Sival has his own room. I think *Tateh* is better at being a doctor than at building houses. Most houses here are built from stone.'

'Our new house is built from stone,' said Aude. She drew her hand from his, feeling oddly shy. 'I think it's just a farmhouse, but my father pretends it's a chateau.'

'I don't suppose we could visit you there,' said Yuda, glancing at his sister, who shook her head.

Aude sighed. She felt an ache inside her chest. 'Mother wouldn't mind, but my father wouldn't allow it,' she said.

'Well he can't tell me what to do, because I'm a man now,' said Yuda. '*Tateh* took us to the Beit in Masalyar last week, and I became Bar Mitzvah. That means 'Son of the Covenant'. I had to stand up in front of the whole community and chant a passage from the Law of the Wanderers. It was scary.'

'*Mameh* and I watched from the women's gallery upstairs,' said Yuste. 'We couldn't see much. But he did it all, without any mistakes.'

'And the next day, Sival took us to the public library. He wanted to see if there was anything in the city records about Savorin. He found a few references to the legend in old books, but nothing to say if it was true.'

'We had to wait with him while the librarian went and searched the stacks for the books he ordered!' said Yuste. 'And we were able to visit the reading room. They have electric light in there so people can stay after dark!'

'We each had a book to look at,' said Yuda.

Aude was less interested in the delights of the library than of hearing about Yuda's Bar Mitzvah.

'What is a Beit like? I've never seen one,' she said. 'I'm not sure what it means.'

'It means 'house' as in House of Prayer,' said Yuda. 'It looks ordinary from the outside. But inside it's... different. There aren't many windows in ours, and it's dark. I had to stand on a raised platform called a Bimah... there are too many words to explain. They took out one of the scrolls and I recited a portion from it. The letters look like the ones you saw... the other day.' He glanced at Aude, who nodded to show she had understood. 'Written in black ink on parchment. The words of formation.'

He stopped talking, and seemed to be gazing inwards.

'It's difficult to describe to a... Doxan,' said Yuste. 'We don't have any images of saints, or the Mother and the Son. The walls are painted plaster, and there are brass chandeliers hanging from the ceiling. And at the back of the room is the Holy Ark where they keep the scrolls. It looks like a cupboard in the wall, with painted and gilded doors. That's the most sacred place in the Beit.'

'I had to lift one of the scrolls,' said Yuda. 'It's heavy. And it's... like a person. I mean, the scroll wears ornate silver crowns on the finials. It's dressed in a velvet cloth, and decorated with a silver breastplate. I could feel the weight of history and words when I was holding it. I felt it could see me, and was looking into my soul.'

'It sounds as if it was alive,' said Aude, giving a little shiver.

The twins looked at each other, sharing *sprechen*.

'Not really,' said Yuste. 'It's the Law of the Wanderers, written down. All the way back to the beginning. When the One gave it to our ancestors in Zyon.'

'We don't speak the name of the One,' said Yuda. He fidgeted, as if the thought made him uncomfortable. 'No-one knows how to say it. In prayer books, it's written as two letters. The true name is too dangerous. When our ancestors lived in Zyon, only the High Priest was allowed to say it.'

'*Zyon*. That must be what we call Outremer. The Land of the Son.'

'It is our land,' said Yuda. He looked angry; angry with her! 'We were driven out. And people mock us because we have no homeland.'

'Yudi,' said his sister, laying her hand on his sleeve. 'That isn't Aude's fault. It was such a long time ago. It's not a shame to be Wanderers.'

'I'm not ashamed,' said Yuda. 'And I know Aude isn't like the others. I never thought all the Dzuzukim were bad. Doxoi. But it's important to remember who we are, and where we come from. If we don't remember, others will.'

Aude knew Yuda was impulsive and moody, in a way that his sister seldom was. But he had been shaking with anger when he talked about Zyon, when to Aude it was only a legendary place, somewhere too far away and long ago to be imagined. She had never

33

questioned what she was taught by the Doxan priests, though the belief of her own mother contradicted it at several points; but neither the Mother and Son nor the Goddess had intervened to save Aude and her friend. They had left her alone, left her to suffer grief and loss; and she could not see any point in gods like that.

***

That night in her bed, Aude dreamed she was walking on the deep sea floor. She had never seen it in real life, except when she had gone swimming in the bay. In the dream, she could breathe underwater without fear of drowning. She had not changed into a mermaid; she could see her own bare feet, changed by the colour of the water.

The ground sloped downwards, and the sky overhead drew further away. Aude trod on pebbles that were really pearls, and started as tiny silver fishes finned past her, so she glimpsed their round eyes for an instant.

Her red hair trailed upwards in the water. Some of the fish that surrounded her had red or golden scales; they were armoured like – myrmidons. Not mermaids. A shoal of tiny warriors, mounted on seahorses, swept past in her imagination.

Here on the sea bed, there were no storms; the water moved slowly, with a wallowing motion, and sea-serpents uncoiled in their sleep, flickering their tongues before falling asleep again. Shipwrecks lay in the distance, crewed by skeletons, their ragged sails still unfurled in the tides; the eyes of the figureheads on the ships prow moved as Aude walked past, watching her go.

Ahead of her lay Savorin. Aude knew she should not go there, but her feet carried her on. High walls built of blue-tinged stone, and windows whose glass had shattered. What catastrophe had drowned the city and left it so far beneath the sea, so long ago that no-one recalled its true name? If she listened carefully, she would hear the bells ringing, calling the people to prayer, though no-one was alive to answer.

Aude woke with a start, her heart pounding in her chest. She remembered the white skull face and the crowned head rising through the surf. How odd that Yuda and Yuste, scrawny and skinny, had seemed so little afraid!

The room door swung open, and her mother's face appeared in the dusk, not quite dawn yet. Since they moved south, she had taken to checking up on Aude, as if she feared her daughter might not be breathing. She seemed to be the only person who understood what

Aude had lost, without blaming her for the family's exile. If anything, Aude thought Aelis had been glad to leave the castle, even though she had lived nowhere else.

'Aude. I thought I heard you cry out.'

Aude moved her hand over her eyes. 'I was dreaming, *Maman*. Dreaming about the sea.'

Aelis sat down on the edge of her bed. 'This is a different place. Here the sea is important, not the forest.'

'Tell me that story again. The one about the Goddess.'

Aelis tugged her shawl round her shoulders. 'You ought to get some sleep,' she said. 'It will be dawn soon and your father will be stirring.'

Aude shrugged. She had little or no feeling for Gaudry, who was always angry. Aelis sighed.

'Very well,' she said. 'The Goddess was one of the Son's female followers, who fled Zyon after the Kadegoi executed him. We have always blamed the Kadegoi for his death rather than the Wanderers because the Kadegin Empire ruled Zyon in those days. The surviving companions sailed to Masalyar. When they landed, they parted company and travelled to different parts of Lefranu. And some came to settle in the forest.'

'Which one became the Goddess? Or are they all her?' said Aude, feeling drowsy.

Her mother laughed. 'Goddesses are complicated,' she said. 'All you need to know is that the one we honour – our goddess – has two aspects, dark and light. She is the Bright Lady or the Cold One, bringer of death and separation. That's not much, for a goddess.'

Aude reached out for her mother's hand. 'But it's just for us. Not father or the boys.'

Aelis nodded. 'Just us. Your father calls it heresy. It is a secret faith, and one practised only amongst friends.'

'May I tell Yuste and Yuda?' said Aude.

Aelis squeezed her hand. 'You cannot tell them, for their lives are already in danger. Some Doxoi kill Wanderers; you know the Seigneur himself talked of it. The children will know by now that you are not a strict Doxan. Or I would not have entered their parents' house and taken tea with their mother. You must remember to treat them with respect and kindness. They have taken a liking to you, but they are vulnerable in ways you are not. Not only Wanderers, but shamans as well.'

'I wish I could have been a shaman,' said Aude.

'No, you do not,' said her mother. 'It is better to live in one world at a time. Don't envy shamans; they have a hard destiny.'

***

Whenever they could not sleep, Yuste and Yuda had developed the habit of climbing out onto the roof of their house, where they had created a small observatory. They called it the Planetarium, which was a grand name for something that consisted of a small telescope and a brass orrery their father had made for them out of old clock parts. He was clever with his hands, and the orrery worked; the sun sat in the centre, and the planets that orbited it were made from glass marbles. The Earth had its own satellite or moon, and was bigger than some of the other planets; the twins called it 'Mir', though they knew the local children called it something different.

They liked to sit on the roof in their nightshirts and watch the sky for constellations and shooting stars. Wanderers had their own names for the constellations, and it was confusing to remember those as well as the official ones taught in lessons. The twins argued without making a sound; they had learned not to start fighting each other, as that would certainly wake their parents or Sival.

They were playing the shamanic equivalent of I-Spy. One of them would give the first letter of a constellation and the other would have to guess it. This required a certain skill when you were sharing each other's thoughts, since it was easy to forget your twin was listening and blurt out the answer. Yuda was something of a blurter. When he made a mistake, he and sister would double up with shared silent laughter. They could not play simple games like paper, scissors, stone because they knew each other's choice beforehand.

'It's no good,' whispered Yuda. 'I must be tired. I can't ward my thoughts.'

It was tacitly admitted between them that Yuste was the clever one. Yuda wasn't stupid, but he was less interested in their lessons, even the ones that were not religious. He and Yuste spent most of their time studying; they had schoolwork, studying the Law of the Wanderers with their father, and learning how to use their powers from Sival. Yuste loved the lessons, and worked hard, and still had time for play, though she also had to help their mother with the housework. Yuda was inattentive, unless Sival was teaching him; he wanted to spend as much time with their Teacher as possible.

– *You'll have to marry a man when you're old enough. Horrible,* he thought.

Yuste would have a marriage arranged for her by a *shadchan*, or match-maker, from Masalyar. Most Wanderer women married between the ages of eighteen and twenty-five; once wed they would be kept busy bearing children and making a home for their husband.

– *You'll have to marry a woman!*

They were sitting side by side with their backs against the chimney stack. It was warm at this time of night because their mother kept the stove lit, though damped down, even in summer.

– *I've never met any other Wanderer girls. Not even when we went to the Beit in Masalyar. They kept their eyes lowered, and they ran away if you tried to speak to them.*

– *I suppose they had to be modest,* thought Yuste. *They have to start practising for when they become women.*

– Mameh *isn't like that.*

They thought of their mother, letting the images travel between their minds. She was younger and less old-fashioned than their father; the twins were more in awe of him, though he never struck them, or Yuste at any rate. Their mother refused to smack them, but she had a fierce temper that could frighten them; their father's quietness was worse.

– *I wish we could stay here. Live here all our lives,* thought Yuda.

– *I wish we could, but we can't. We're not children any more. You've had your bar mitzvah, and I have had my...* she stopped, shy of thinking the word.

He nodded. Though they still shared a bedroom, their parents had hung a curtain down the middle to preserve their separation, and when Yuste had her period, she had to sleep in a separate room, which was complicated. Yuda sometimes thought the Law of the Wanderers had been invented to make their lives difficult. There were so many rules, and because they were the only Wanderers for miles, they stood out even more.

– Tateh *wants me to be a Rashim or a scribe. And I don't want to!*

– *Has he been talking about that again? But you will go and live in Masalyar at the Yeshiva!*

– *I don't want to study at the Yeshiva. I want to use my powers. We may be the first Wanderers born with powers! And* Tateh *doesn't like us to use them.*

Yuste gave a shrug. – *Some people think Wanderers are magical anyway.* Tateh *doesn't want to draw attention to us.*

– *It's too late for that.* Her brother stood up restlessly. – *We look different, we sound different and we eat different food. Nobody at school understands why I won't eat saucisson sec! They understand us not eating pork but there's nothing wrong with sausage.*

– Tateh *says we shouldn't make friends with Dzuzuk children.*

This was a sore point. They had already made friends with Dzuzuk children. Since they started attending the local school, they had found oddities and outsiders to befriend, and formed their own gang. Yuda was the leader of the gang, and Yuste was his second in command; the gang members looked out for each other, offering mutual protection from the school bullies or any of the older children who decided to attack outsiders.

There was Cricri, the son of a Darkman from Morea; Gustave, tall, fat and shambling, who wore thick spectacles and was slow in class; and lame François, the son of a fisherman who could not forgive his son for his weak leg. Cricri suffered because he was dark-skinned, and illegitimate. The five of them had sworn an oath of friendship, and they had a password and a secret sign. Their headquarters was the sea-cave where Yuste and Yuda had taken Aude, because they knew most local children were superstitious about the beach.

Yuda knew, and had known for some time, even before his bar mitzvah, that he could not follow the path his father had mapped out for him. He had no idea what he was going to do, or how to avoid it; he was a Wanderer, and sons obeyed their fathers. Though *Mameh* had taught him and his sister music, and said they were good at it, there was no question of respectable Wanderer children becoming itinerant musicians.

Yuste came to stand beside her brother. She wanted what he wanted; but she wished her father would let her study to be a scribe, instead of expecting her to marry someone she hardly knew, just as he had been married to their mother when they arrived in Masalyar as exiles from Sklava. It had been a marriage arranged by the community, since bride and groom had left their families behind to travel to the west. And though their parents seemed affectionate, there was a gulf between them because they had grown up in such different households: Kayla in a modernising household in Maskovi, and Mordechai in a traditional, pious family in Ades.

– *You know girls can't be scribes. Or Rashmi. And since we live outside the community, we have to set an example.*

Yuda was repeating what their father had said to them many times. Since they were the only Wanderers in the area, they must deal justly with the strangers among whom they lived, and show that their people were honourable, honest and righteous. Neither Yuda nor Yuste found this easy; their father's moral standards were high, and he expected his family to show the same sense of duty and piety. They had to dress modestly, which wasn't difficult since Wanderers were only allowed to wear black and white, or brown as a concession; but there seemed to be so many other rules, a new one every day, about what they were allowed to eat and who they were allowed to touch.

Yuda should not have touched Aude. They had tried not to mention it, but it had leaked out, and their father had looked grave. Yuste and Yuda hardly needed to think how glad they were that he was not a shaman and would never know that Aude had been naked. And they had wasted a lot of effort trying not to look at her while being fascinated because her skin was pale, and freckled.

– *I wish we could run away. A long way from home, maybe to the city. We could earn our living as musicians.* Yuda contradicted his earlier thought, and Yuste did not remind him.

– *We couldn't live outside the community. And the elders would tell our parents where we were.*

– *We'd have to hide somewhere they couldn't find us. We'd let Sival know but no-one else, apart from the gang.*

– *We'd never survive in Masalyar. The city is a dangerous place. We might be kidnapped and sold into slavery.*

– *I can't stay here, Yuste.*

Yuste leaned her head on his shoulder. She sometimes wondered why they were their parents' only children. Most Wanderers had big families, and lived surrounded by uncles, aunts and cousins, who helped with the child-rearing. Kaila had given birth to them when she was twenty, and had born no children since; they were too shy to ask why not, but they wondered. Everyone else they knew, apart from Cricri, had lots of brothers and sisters.

– *You could ask Sival,* her brother thought.

– *When we reach sixteen, he will return to the city and found a college there. Then what will we do?*

– *We'll have to go with him.*

Yuste sighed, and wiped her nose on her sleeve. – Mameh *and* Tateh *will never let us. I will be married, and you will attend the Yeshiva.*

Yuda pulled a face. He had visited the Yeshiva with his father on the day he was bar mitzvah, and seen rows of boys, of all heights and ages, sitting on benches bent over the books of the Law. Some were chanting, rocking to and fro as they read the holy words. And he had been the only shaman in the room; everyone else was Teshvet, like his father and mother. He had been desperate to find his sister and share his thoughts with her before his brain exploded.

– *It looked boring. And the building smelled of boiled cabbage.*

– *But you'd be surrounded by Wanderers! Not Dzuzukim, like here.*

– *Our friends are Dzuzukim. Aude is.*

– *I know...*

Sadness moved between them; a constriction in the throat, the beginning of tears in their eyes. What they wanted most was to stay together and to remain children; they knew their bodies were changing, and before long there would be sensations that needed to be hidden or kept private. Though they were not identical twins, they could not imagine separating, not even for a day. That was what truly frightened them; they could see how their lives would diverge, and had already begun to diverge.

It was Yuda who had gone to the Beit in Masalyar to recite a portion of the Law in front of the congregation. Yuste and their mother had sat upstairs in the women's gallery, hidden by a pierced screen. Reb Mordechai had been downstairs listening to his son, together with the other men of the community.

Yuste had peeped through the openings in the screen to watch as her brother was called to the Bimah. He had looked even more scrawny and small than usual. He still looked like a little boy, and she had changed, and was changing, into a woman; she had developed puny breasts, pubic hair, and lots of other dark hair that sprouted from awkward places. Yuste did not want to think about what was going to happen to her brother. Their mother had talked to each of them in private, to explain these changes, which she called puberty.

They had watched the wave of adolescence passing over their classmates. Yuste had been one of the first girls to change, which was horrible. Suddenly she had to be careful, and worry about menstrual blood, and keep herself clean. She suffered from cramps, and had to wear special pieces of cloth tied with a belt that no-one else must see. And as a Wanderer, she had to take a ritual bath in the sea once her period ended; until then she was *Niddah*, which meant unclean.

Now the boys in their year had started to reach puberty. Gustave was one; his mother told theirs that he had outgrown his strength, being tall and stout. Voices broke, the boys started to grow in height, and the girls heard them laughing together in groups; it seemed other body parts had started to get bigger too.

Yuda did not join in these communal sessions, because he had not changed yet. And amongst their gang, Gustave was the only one who had begun. Despite his size, he was bullied by the other boys, because he was fat and slow. Yuda, Cricri and François struggled to defend him, because they were all skinny and small for their age. Yuda would have liked to use his powers, but Sival had put a block on them.

The twins did not know when Yuda would change, but they had an inkling it would be soon. A shaman's power signature or durmat changed colour when they reached puberty. When they were little, their durmats had been blue, then blue-green; Sival explained that adolescence would make them change to silver, possibly overnight.

– *I don't want to be a man,* Yuda thought.

– *I don't think you have much choice, Yudi.*

– *It would be all right if I could be tall, like* Tateh. *But I'm never going to be tall. Sival said.*

– *Sival isn't tall himself, and it would be okay to be like him.*

– *I suppose so. It's just that I'm scared, Yuste. I won't be me any more. Not this me.*

– *I'm still me!*

He glanced at her, hesitantly. She knew what he was thinking: ritual baths, rules of modesty, being *Niddah*. Yuste was already a Wanderer woman, a state that carried different rules and burdens to being a Wanderer man. The two of them were being prised apart by forces beyond their control, and not just the changes in their bodies. The twins were well aware that their religion prized men above women. Women were precious jewels whose modesty and honour had to be protected; they were not full members of the community for the purposes of the Law.

The twins knew how much these rules had chafed their mother. Yuste wondered if that was one reason why their father had moved from the city to the rural areas; not just to work as a doctor where one was needed, but to protect their mother from coming into conflict with the more conservative women in Masalyar. Or to stop her disgracing him? This thought was difficult to bear. Yuste loved Reb Mordechai, but as she grew up she had noticed the rigidity in his outlook. He did believe girls should be educated, and allowed to study the Law; but their destiny was to be wives and mothers, to set up and keep a Clean home, and to bear children.

41

It was turning cold, and reluctantly Yuste and Yuda returned to their bedroom and the sheet that divided it. They called it the 'Mechitzah' after the barrier that separated men from women in some houses of worship. The barrier did not keep their minds apart, but it reminded them of the thoughts that had been troubling them all evening.

'I'm worried about Savorin,' said Yuda. 'I think it's awake.'

Yuste wriggled under the covers. 'We haven't noticed anything since that day.'

'I keep having shaman's dreams about it. And I saw Aude there.'

'You went there in dreams?'

'I couldn't help it. I found myself there, outside the sunken city. I couldn't get inside, but I couldn't leave either. I was walking round the walls, looking for a gate, and I saw Aude in the distance. I don't think she saw me.'

'Aude isn't a shaman,' said Yuste, flatly.

'I know that. But I think she's been affected by magic. There's a sort of shadow round her. It's not a durmat; it's something I've never seen before.'

'Do you think she's a witch?'

Yuda laughed, so much Yuste thought he would choke. 'She can't be a witch if she isn't a shaman! But I think magic leaves a trace. A proper shaman would be able to detect it.'

Yuste sat up in bed, swung her legs over the side and got up to peep round the curtain edge. She couldn't see her brother clearly in the dark, but she could see his durmat if she closed his eyes. Was she imagining it, or had the colour started to change?

'You shouldn't go there,' she whispered. 'We were warned against it.'

Yuda peeped over the edge of the covers at her. 'When I was little, I used to hope I'd find treasure. Piles of gold, and jewels, and magical harps. They say that the halls of the city are filled with riches.'

Yuste shuddered. 'And with skeletons guarding them. Skulls everywhere. I don't want cursed treasure, Yudi.'

'I don't want it, but I'd like to see it. Like the fabled crown of the last king of Lefranu. They say it's kept at the Doxan Dom in Rins, waiting for the next king to be crowned – if he ever returns.'

'I hope he never returns. He'd only pass more laws against Wanderers. He might even try to expel us. I don't want there to be another Doxan king.'

42

She crept back to her bed, and got under the covers; she was getting cold. And as soon as she wanted to, she fell asleep – and had a shaman's dream, which she had not asked for.

***

Aude found herself near the sunken city again. This time, it was not dark; sunlight struggled down through the water, which rippled and swung about her as she walked. And the ancient walls gleamed; though there was weed growing from their ramparts, and from gaps in the rock, she could see in her mind's eye the city that had been lost, before it sank beneath the waves. The mighty stones shone in the daylight, the sea was blue in the distance, and the sky was clear.

Aude walked up to the wall. She was no longer afraid, only curious; that day when the storm had brought terror from the sea seemed long ago. She touched the stone, wondering whether Savorin had been the city's true name. It sounded like a name conferred by legend; she was sure she had read stories of a similar place in the far west, off the coast of Aquitaine, another part of Lefranu cut off during the Great Cold.

She wondered how easy it would be to get inside the city. If she was only dreaming, why did everything feel so real? She turned to her left and followed the course of the wall, keeping her right hand on the stone. Up above her, shoals of fish passed like shadows, and jellyfish bobbed on the tide. They looked so pretty when the light caught them that it was easy to forget how they could sting the skin.

A shaman would know what to do in a place like this. Aude thought of the twins, and wondered whether they ever came here. It was difficult to believe that either of them possessing tremendous powers: shy and skinny and awkward, they reminded her of wading birds such as curlew and snipe.

On her first day at the local school, the twins had introduced her to their friends. Her brother Thibault had tried to make a nuisance of himself, but Aude had ignored him. He was the only one of her brothers young enough to attend school.

At break time, he had caught her arm, pinching her hard. In spite of herself, Aude cried out.

'Papa says we are not to speak to Wanderers. They are accursed. I'll tell on you if you do it again.'

Aude wrenched her arm free, fury giving her strength. 'You tell him – and I'll tell on you! I saw you try to kiss the kitchen maids, the Villandry girls. And you were pinching their bottoms!'

43

Thibault turned red. He mouthed a curse word at her, and lumbered away. Aude watched him go, rubbing her arm and trying not to cry.

It had started already. Children running up to her, pulling or touching her hair and running away.

'Red hair! Red hair! She's a witch.'

The Wanderers and their little gang of outcasts seemed a good place for her to hide. Apart from Gustave, all were short and thin. Cricri had skin the colour of conkers, and curly hair. Aude had never met any Darkmen, and hoped she was not staring too much. François, who had to use a crutch because of his bad leg, was the brains of the group, with a wide smile and brown eyes.

Aude felt sorry for Gustave. He had grown so fat he could hardly see out of his eyes, and his height and bulk had not made him strong. He shambled after the others like a lost dog that had decided to choose new owners. The others ignored him much of the time, and occasionally teased him, but they were not unkind. Each of them had a disadvantage that left them vulnerable at school, where there were children from all over the district, not just Sankt Eglis; it was the big boys of fourteen and older who were most likely to pick on them, though there were girl bullies too.

As it was Aude's first day, Yuste had taken her in charge. She had introduced Aude to some girls in their year and warned her which ones to avoid. Though there were several groups she needed to be wary of, the principal enemies were the gang led by Elise (a tall girl who swept by them with barely a glance), and the Baudoin brothers, Olivier and Pierre, great muscular, overweight louts who reminded Aude of bull-calves.

It seemed important that Elise was a bourgeois, daughter of the town Mayor, while the Baudoin brothers were the sons of a landowner, farmers who would inherit their father's land. Their father was at the top of the pecking order amongst the country-folk, and determined to keep things that way. It meant that the brothers might take unwelcome notice of Aude because her father was a farmer himself, and a stranger to the area.

'They don't often bother you in school,' whispered Yuste. 'They pick on you when you're going home, or when you're alone. Olivier Baudoin was the one who took off Yuda's trousers. They beat him up from time to time.'

Apart from after school, the gang was able to meet up at break times and at lunch, when the children poured of the school buildings into the yard. Aude noticed that many of the older schoolgirls brought knitting or crochet to work on during the lunch-hour, while others played at skipping or jump-rope.

There was a fairly strict separation between the male and female sides of the playground, with teachers on hand to enforce it, but the gang had their own territory at the edge of the school yard, where they would meet to plan their exploits and share any gossip or warnings about the pupils who made their lives difficult. Except for Gustave and François, they were all fast runners, and they needed to be.

They gathered together in a huddle, the girls with their white aprons over their everyday clothes, and the boys uncomfortable in stiff serge jackets. The poorer boys, Cricri and François, wore breeches that had been mended many times, torn shirts and faded jackets that were too tight. They had to go barefoot sometimes.

And Aude remembered. Yuda had been talking about Savorin. The place where she was right now! They all sat cross-legged in a circle apart from him; he was kneeling, sitting back on his knees, something Yuste said he had learnt from their teacher, Sival.

'Yuste and I think Savorin is awake,' he said. Yuste nodded, looking solemn. She had explained to Aude that the rest of the gang already knew about their adventure; she and Yuda told them everything.

Gustave covered his mouth with his hand; Cricri drew the sign of the Wheel on his forehead.

'I don't suppose it was ever asleep,' said François in his reedy voice. 'My mother says that, in grandfather's time, sailors would avoid that part of the bay. They said the city used to take people. Lure them there with tales of treasure and lights under the water. They never came back.'

'I thought the legend was hundreds of years old,' said Cricri.

'Older than anyone can remember,' said Gustave.

'We went swimming out there, and we never saw anything,' said Yuda. 'But there is something. I keep dreaming I'm under the sea, just outside the city walls...'

Aude stopped remembering and looked around. She was here, now, with her eyes open, outside the walls of the sunken city! She could see the surface of the sea far above, the wallowing light and the drifting seaweed. But this was the second time she had visited Savorin in her dreams, and now she was standing near the walls, and looking for a gate.

It must be beautiful inside. Nothing had faded with the years; rich silks shimmered in the salt water, and piles of silver and gold plate were heaped high. Jewels winked from the inner recesses of skulls that had once worn them, and fish became jewels themselves. A harp stood where the minstrel had dropped it, with the water playing its strings; a harp made from gold. Aude wanted to pick it up, and set it on her lap, to see whether she could make it sing again. She had been a harper, when she lived at the castle; she had played the harp and sung, as if she were one of the ancient minstrels.

This land, southern Lefranu, which the Kadegoi named Provincia, had been famous for its troubadours: men who wandered from castle to castle, singing songs and telling stories, in the days when the world was free. Aude felt tears running down her face. Those songs had been sung here, in Savorin, with such longing and melancholy; but the sea had swept them away, the lords and the minstrels, the ladies and the servants, until all that remained was a memory and a dark legend.

Aude leaned her cheek against the rough stone. 'I will do it,' she whispered. 'I will set you free, if I can.'

Someone touched her arm, and she turned round to see Yuste standing beside her, her eyes wide and staring. The dark girl's hair streamed loose in the water, and she stared at Aude in fear and recognition.

'What are you doing here, Audie?'

Aude reached out to touch Yuste's cheek. She felt shy of saying anything; it was as if the city had spoken to her in secret.

'I'm dreaming,' she said.

'But you're not a shaman!'

'The city called to me, and I came.'

Yuste threw her arms round her, and hugged her tight, in a paroxysm of fear. And Aude hugged her back, wondering what it was that could frighten someone so powerful.

***

The following day did not dawn well. Yuste woke to find her period had started, and had to call out to her mother for help. Kaila came running with her stock of cloths and safety pins, and helped Yuste to fit them in place. Then she sat and hugged her daughter, who was weeping because of the cramps.

'It's not fair!' Yuste sobbed. 'Yuda doesn't have to put up with anything like this.'

'Yuda will have problems of his own,' said her mother. 'Boys don't get off that lightly.'

Yuste became aware that her brother was absent; he had not been there when she woke up.

'Where is Yudi?' she said.

Kaila hugged her. 'He may be aware of your trouble,' she said. 'He seems to be aware of most things. And between you and me, I think he has already started.'

'What do you mean, *Mameh*?'

Kaila shook her head. 'That was one reason we put up the Mechitzah,' she said, using the twins' name for the sheet. 'It wasn't just to protect your modesty. Yudi's body is changing too. I don't think he likes it. And Sival has warned me it can be more difficult for shamans. I need to discuss this with your father.'

Yuste did not like the sound of anything that had to be discussed with their father. She snuggled up to Kaila, wondering what it was Sival had told her. Kaila stroked her hair.

'You are growing into a woman and Yudi into a man. But you will always keep something of the other opposite sex in you. And it is likely that, whatever the Law of the Wanderers says, you will fall in love with women as well as men. Not all shamans are like that, but many are. Your father will not accept this, and will enjoin you to exercise self-control, but it is easy for him to say. Sival has talked to me at length about this.'

'But maybe we won't feel like that. I don't want to feel like that! I'm happy as I am.'

'Of course, Yustka. But a child cannot remain a child. You are no longer a little girl, and Yuda is starting to change from being a young boy.'

Yuste dressed slowly. It was not like her brother to get up and leave without telling her. She thought of her dream last night, when she had met Aude outside the walls of Savorin. A shaman's dream, and Aude had been there! But neither of them had seen Yuda.

When Yuste had put on all her clothes apart from her outdoor shoes, she lifted the sheet dividing the room and looked over to his side. To her surprise, she found that the bed had been stripped, and the blankets folded at the far end. For one terrible moment, Yuste felt she would faint. She thought her brother had gone for ever, sent away to the Yeshiva before dawn, too early for her to say goodbye. Her father must have made the decision without consulting her or her mother, and Yuda had been obliged to obey.

She leaned on the bed frame, feeling dizzy. The thought of losing her twin's company made her feel sick. It had never seemed to matter

47

that he was a boy and she a girl. She knew what her parents thought, and outsiders, apart from Sival; but Yuda and she did everything together, and always had done.

The room door opened, and her brother entered. He saw where she was at once, and understood why she was crying; he came and put his arms round her, though he was probably not meant to touch her when she was *Niddah*, even though he was her brother.

Yuste howled.

– *I thought you had gone. I thought they had sent you away.*

– *Not yet. No. I had to go out because there was an embarrassing thing with my – thingy.*

He hid his face in her shoulder, and Yuste felt his chagrin as acutely as her own distress. She was not sure what he meant, but she could guess. It had been talked about at school, in the playground. It was one of those things you were not supposed to mention if you were a girl; but girls had brothers.

– *What do you mean?*

– *You remember when we first met Aude, and she had no clothes on? And the light seemed to surround her. In the dream, she walked towards me holding out her hand and smiling. I wanted to touch her skin, it looked so soft, and a pretty colour, like the inside of a shell. I wanted to put my arms round her and squeeze her tight, and never let go. And I wanted to kiss her mouth...*

He stopped. Yuste sensed his distress, alongside another feeling, one he did not have a name for. She patted his back. He was so thin, the bones in his spine and his ribs stood out.

– *I understand,* she thought, but did not know whether that was true.

Yuda drew away from her. – *That was when it happened. I woke up and the sheets were all wet and...horrible. I thought I'd wet the bed like we used to when we were small. But it was something else...*

Though he did not voice his thought, Yuste understood what he meant; he was too embarrassed to think it. Her mouth dropped open; her mother had been right – her brother was changing, in his own way.

– Mameh *told me to go and immerse myself in the sea, the way you do,* he thought. *But she says in future I only have to clean myself and say a blessing. It's not forbidden.*

In spite of herself, Yuste giggled. It was comforting that her brother had his own troubles, though at least he was not ritually impure for days, as she was. It had seemed for a time as if being an adolescent girl was the worst thing in the world.

– *It's not funny! I was having impure thoughts. About Aude.*

Yuste only laughed more; if nothing else, because her brother's description of his dream had been so vague. She had to tell him the truth.

– *Oh Yudi. That was my dream. Exactly the same! I had a shaman's dream first, about meeting Aude outside the walls of Savorin. Even though she isn't a shaman, it was definitely her. And it seemed to be daylight, it was so strange. But afterwards, I had a different dream. Just like the one you describe. I think you must have shared my dream.*

Yuda folded his arms and scowled. – *That's not possible. You're a girl.*

– *Of course it's possible! Sival told us, and* Mameh *says the same thing.*

He stepped away from her, frowning at her. Yuste felt suddenly sick; drowned in anger black as tar.

– *You can't have her! She's mine. I'm going to marry her* –

And he stormed out of the room, tearing down the curtain as he went, and leaving Yuste with tears burning her eyes.

***

It was a school day, but Aude's elder brothers and her father had been up before dawn, riding out to survey their estates. They came in as she, her mother and Thibault were sitting down at the big kitchen table, made to feast a whole household after the vendange. Aude still thought of them as knights, and traces of their old costume remained, in the fine leather boots and polished spurs they wore to ride out, even when they were only visiting the farm. They often carried arms as well, not the modern guns they despised, but short swords and bows that were easy to carry and could be readily hidden.

Aude always felt a thrill of fear in her father's presence. She was expected to stand when he entered a room, along with Thibault and their mother. He never let them forget that he had been a feudal lord, and they were his vassals. He might not be a Seigneur in the south, but he intended to maintain his rights and privileges at home, over his family and his servants.

Gaudry gave them leave to sit down, and helped himself to wine and white bread from the buffet. Once again, Aude had to wait until he had begun to eat before she could resume her meal. Her mother had discovered coffee since they moved to Sankt Eglis, and ensured that

49

one of the kitchen maids prepared bowls and a full jug for herself, Aude and Thibault. She did not approve of her husband drinking wine to break his fast, but at the castle there had been little else, apart from the detestable small beer, which tasted sour and smelled like piss, as Thibault had once complained.

Her father was addressing her. Aude shivered. She kept her gaze on her plate.

'So, Mademoiselle, how do you find this new-fangled school to which we have sent you? Do you profit from it? I hope you have not learnt any low habits from mingling with peasants and the bourgeoisie.'

'No, Mon Seigneur. I am learning how to read Kadegin, together with rhetoric and geometry.'

'A waste of time, teaching girls. But your mother will have her way. And how about you, Thibault? Have you become a scholar, since it seems you are fit for little else?'

Aude might dislike her brother, but she felt her cheeks burn in sympathy.

Thibault glanced at Gaudry, and she saw a flash of hate in his eyes. 'I attend classes every day, Mon Seigneur, and do my studies. But I am a man, and it irks me to sit on a bench with children, reciting sums and memorising words.'

Gaudry gave a short laugh, like a fox's bark. 'You have to learn because when you reach your majority, and not before, I will need someone to do the accounts of the farm, and keep records. I think you will be good enough for that. As for your sister, I fear too much learning may spoil her, and make her even more unfit for a good marriage. But perhaps we will find someone in these parts willing to take her, in spite of her cursed hair.'

Aude's older brothers laughed noisily. Her hair was a joke, since nobody else in the family had a hint of such redness. When she was younger, Thibault had told her she must be a changeling. None of them really believed that red hair was cursed, but they knew some men would refuse to marry a redhead, since it was a colour attributed to witches.

'Well, Mon Seigneur, I hope you have finished teasing your youngest,' said Aelis, putting down her napkin. 'You gave your consent that Aude and Thibault should attend the local school, rather than being taught at home by a tutor or a governess. Have you had ill reports of their behaviour from the teachers or other parents?'

Gaudry tore the bread with his teeth. He pointed the remaining piece at Aude.

'That child... spends too much time with the Wanderers. I do not like it.'

Aelis shook her head. 'Of course she does. They must be the only children she knows in the whole district. In time, she will meet others, and make more friends.'

Aude stole a glance at Thibault and saw from his bemused expression that he must have kept his promise. She did not think him clever enough to pretend innocence. If he had told on her to their father, he would be smiling and gloating over her distress. Instead, he looked puzzled, and perhaps afraid she would tell Gaudry of his misdemeanours with the Villandry girls.

'I do not like it,' Gaudry repeated. 'I want her raised in Doxa. For her to fraternise with Wanderers brings shame on our house. It has been noticed. Today, on my rounds, I met with Monsieur Baudoin, who is first amongst the local landowners, and whose estates exceed even our own. He chaffed me, saying his sons had noticed our daughter making sport with the twins – for there are two, a boy and a girl – and not only are they Wanderers, but shamans! Though they do not use their powers at the school, the fact is notorious in the neighbourhood. They have a teacher, a sorcerer from Inde, who lives at their house and trains them up in the Black Arts. Baudoin says he has carnal knowledge of the mother...'

He did not finish, for Aelis sprang to her feet. She banged her plate on the table.

'Gaudry d'Iforas! Mother forbid you should use such language in front of the children. Whatever gossip you may hear, keep it to yourself, or share it with your cronies. I met Madame Vasilyevich, and she seemed a respectable and modest woman. I also met with the *sorcerer* from Inde, and he was courteous and well-spoken. I made no inquiries about his religion, but he spoke Franj as well as you or I. I am shocked to hear you slander an honest woman in such terms. She may be a Wanderer, but she has done you no wrong.'

'You should not berate me so disrespectfully, woman,' said Gaudry. He did not stand up, but his voice was low and threatening. He hardly ever struck their mother, but Aude knew he regarded it as his right.

Aelis sat down at the table once more, straightening the veil that covered her head. Her cheeks were flushed with anger.

'Forgive me, my Lord,' she said in a voice that dripped irony. 'I forgot myself. I do not know this Monsieur Baudoin. Have you encountered his sons at the school, Thibault?'

'I'll say I did!' said Thibault. 'There's one in the senior class and one in the year below. Big, sturdy louts, with more brawn than brain. They have dark hair and tanned skin after the manner of the Southerners. On the first day, they wanted to know who I was, and what business I had at their school. They made fun of my accent and my manner of speech, saying I sounded like a Northerner, and that I spoke like an old book. They said they would like a word with me.'

'It sounds as if they would challenge you to a fight,' said Gaudry. 'You should not accept such a challenge from someone so far beneath you in rank.'

'I may not have much choice,' said Thibault, glancing at his knuckles, and Aude guessed he had already been in a fight with the Baudoin brothers. She warmed to him for the first time in a long while. He had not told tales on her, and he had tried to deal with the Baudoins himself, rather than complaining to Gaudry.

Gaudry gave a short laugh again. 'Well, well,' he said. 'Perhaps you have something of my mettle in you after all. It seems these boys must have gone crying to their father, when they found you less easy to subdue than they thought.'

Thibault nodded, examining his skinned knuckles. 'I shouldn't think they liked the way I answered them,' he said, half to himself.

***

Yuda was half way to school before he stopped and thought over what had happened. He stopped and sat down with his back to the hedgerow, and hid his face against his knees. He was crying because he had shouted at Yuste and because, worse still, she had laughed at him. She did not understand how horrible it was to wake up and find your body had done something in the night without consulting you.

He had noticed changes in his private parts for more than a year now. Nothing pronounced, but enough to make him uneasy. There was no-one to ask apart from his mother, whom he was too ashamed to talk to, or Sival, who had tried to reassure him. There was no question of him talking to his father; Mordechai was a shy, reserved man who was slow to anger, but also slow to show affection to his son. He seemed uncertain how to talk to Yuda, and more at ease with Yuste; but Yuda carried the burden of all his hopes. And the boy knew, and had known for some time, that he was unequal to them.

It was bad luck that had given his sister the perfect character for studying and learning. She loved reading as much as playing outdoors or swimming in the bay. Yuda loved it too, but he did not want to spend hours poring over books of the Law, or arguing points of interpretation with his father. And now he was beginning to show all the awkward signs of growing into a man.

The Law forbade masturbation, and discouraged pious men from touching their member even to urinate, something Yuda found ridiculous. He knew that when he used the urinals at school, the other boys were always curious because he had been circumcised. He had compared notes with Cricri, Francois and even Gustave, and they had all agreed that they were puny. The differences in appearance fascinated them, and François had been known as 'fuzzy balls' for a while, a term of endearment they had been forced to drop as they caught up with him.

The worst thing was to be further from Yuste than he had ever been in his life. She was *Niddah* as long as her period lasted; some Rashim argued that even a brother should not touch his sister at such a time. It felt as if someone had taken a wooden wedge and hammered it between them, splitting them at the root. Yuste had become a woman, and Yuda was meant to recite a prayer every day thanking the One that he had not been born female. The words made him shake with anger.

He picked up his satchel, slung it across his shoulders and mooched on down the road to the schoolhouse. There was still some way to go, and he did not want to be late and risk a caning from the headteacher. He had been practising biting his lip to stop himself crying out, because it made him so angry that the teachers should strike him, or anyone else. He dreamed of snatching the cane from their hands and breaking it over his knee, but he lacked the strength to do so. It was the injustice that irked him, and the feeling that no adult should have such power over a child.

Walking down into a dip where the road descended into a valley before climbing the other side, he was set upon by Olivier Baudoin, who had been lying in wait behind a wayside shrine. Olivier was the size of a full-grown man, and it took little effort for him to wrestle Yuda to the ground, punching and kicking him as they fell. Yuda felt the punches slamming into the side of his head, and feared Olivier would break his skull. He tried to fight back, but his strength was that of a boy, without Olivier's muscles or his weight.

53

'Let go of me!' he shouted.

Olivier gave a slobbering laugh in his ear, and his hands began to fumble with the buckle of Yuda's belt. And Yuda remembered stories he had heard, that Olivier liked to rape those he overpowered, not because he fancied men but because it showed he was powerful and they were no better than women.

The thought of being used like this was intolerable to Yuda. He jabbed Olivier in the ribs with his knee, and tried to kick him in the groin. Olivier was used to fighting, but he was not accustomed to the weak fighting back. He managed to avoid the impact of Yuda's well-aimed kick, but it sent him sprawling backwards onto his heels. Shaking with rage and fright, Yuda staggered to his feet, refastening his belt. He saw a flash of sunlight on metal and realised that Olivier was coming at him with a knife.

Thoughts rushed through Yuda's mind, images and cries of terror. He could see the blade of the knife and imagine the cold feeling as it pierced his gut. Things had gone too far. Perhaps Olivier had believed that, if he was able to overpower Yuda and rape him, the smaller boy would have been too ashamed to tell anyone. Perhaps Olivier had done this before. But Yuda had fought him off, and he was a Wanderer, the Doctor's son; he could not be relied on to keep the code of silence, because he was already an outcast. He might report what Olivier had done to the teachers; and then it was a crime, one for which Olivier could be flogged, and worse.

Yuda had never thought more quickly. He knew Olivier meant to kill him, or maim him so badly he would never tell anyone what had happened. He was not strong enough to fight Olivier off, and he was sure, beaten and bruised, that he could not outrun the other boy. As Olivier lunged at him, he jumped and rolled, turning a somersault. And as he came up from the somersault, catching Olivier off guard, he raised his left hand and sent a long stream of anger and fear down his arm, burning and bubbling; all the pent-up rage and fear from the years when the Baudoin brothers had tormented him and his sister and their friends.

There was a bright light, bright as the sun in his eyes, and a loud bang. Yuda was thrown to the ground, and he felt a searing pain in the palm of his left hand, as if the skin had been torn off in one go. He was blinded by the flash of light, but he heard a terrible scream, somewhere between a howl and a cry, that scarcely sounded human. When he could open his eyes, he saw something staggering away, a man on fire, burning as he ran; then he fell and lay on the ground, still burning, and there was a smell that made Yuda vomit.

He must have lost consciousness. He woke with his head in someone's lap, and Yuste bending over him, crying. She was pouring water into his mouth from a glass bottle, and she leapt back as he gasped and spluttered. He felt a cool hand on his forehead.

'Hush, hush,' said Madame d'Iforas. 'You are safe.'

His left hand seemed to be burning, but it was wrapped in the most wonderful, cool ointment and light bandages, so light they could have been made by elves. He found Aude and Yuste either side of him, their faces red and blotchy with tears.

'We thought you were dead! We thought he had killed you,' said Aude, sobbing.

Yuda thought of the burning horror he had seen trying to run from him. 'Where is he?' he said.

'They've taken him away. What's left of him,' said Aelis, signing herself with the Wheel. She sighed. 'There will be an inquest. But when we found you, with his knife on the ground close by, and the blows to your face and body... it was clear you acted in self-defence.'

'He was going to kill me,' said Yuda. He felt himself starting to shake. He did not know how he would ever forget the sight of that burning, howling figure, lurching away from him. He had done that, without trying. And Yuste could see the thoughts in his mind. He saw her changing colour, turning pale. 'He tried to rape me,' he said, and sobbed.

'Alas, poor child,' said Aelis. 'Of course, his father will demand reparations of some kind.'

'Madame, everyone knew about Olivier,' said Yuste. 'He used his... member... to show his power over younger boys. Especially if he thought they were weak.'

'I couldn't let him do that to me,' said Yuda. 'And then he tried to kill me.'

'We found you here, lying by the road, and him further off,' said Yuste. She gave a shiver. 'He was burnt to the bone. Aude ran to fetch her mother, and Thibault went on to the school to alert them and send for a stretcher. He told us he'd heard Olivier uttering threats against you. He has been very good.'

'I killed a man. I gave in to the *Yetser Hara*,' said Yuda. He began to cry.

'He means the "evil impulse", said Yuste to Aelis and Aude. 'But even our father will understand that he acted in self-defence.'

Yuda tried to lift his left hand, swathed in bandages. He knew he was suffering from power-burn, something that afflicted inexperienced shamans who used their powers in a fight for the first time. He did not understand how he could have overridden the block Sival had put in his mind.

Yuste dabbed at his forehead and cheek with a damp cloth. 'You're burning up,' she said. 'You have a fever. But I think the block Sival put on your powers must have given way. And that's not the only thing...'

She stopped speaking, because their father had arrived. He looked as tall as a pine tree in his long black frock coat, with his broad-brimmed hat pulled down over his forehead. He wore dark-rimmed spectacles, but Yuda knew his father's eyes were a deep black, the same colour as his own.

'*Meine zun,*' said Reb Mordechai. And without warning, he bent over and scooped Yuda up in his arms as if he were a small child. Yuda realised, with dismay, that there were tears on his father's face. He heard Reb Mordechai murmur a blessing over him, thanks for deliverance from danger.

'I'm sorry, *Tateh,*' he whispered. 'I disobeyed you.'

To his surprise, Reb Mordechai smiled at him. 'Never mind that, Yudeleh,' he said. 'I'm going to take you home.' He turned to Madame D'Iforas, who had risen to her feet, and was standing waiting for him to speak, with the two girls clinging together beside her. Yuda was surprised to hear his father speak with genuine warmth.

'Thank you, Madame D'Iforas, for your kindness to a Wanderer and a stranger,' he said. 'You and your daughter will always be welcome at our house. Your son Thibault too.'

Yuda saw Aelis smile. She bobbed a curtsey, which was the polite response when a gentleman paid you a compliment. He glimpsed her, watching them leave, as his father carried him back along the road towards the Vasilyevich House.

***

In the days that followed, the surviving Baudoin brother was not seen at school again. As Yuste had said, a lot of history came out about the older brother's fondness for assaulting younger boys; it seemed he had forced one or two girls as well. Nonetheless, there was a scandal, and much excitement, that the little Wanderer had used his powers against the son of a local worthy; it took some diplomacy on the part of Reb Mordechai, Madame D'Iforas, and the village priest, to diffuse the anger.

During that time, Aude and Yuste went to school arm in arm, and Thibault escorted them everywhere. He became an unofficial member of the gang, though it was understood that Yuda would have the last word when he returned to school. It became clear he was gravely ill; not just with the power burn that had seared his left hand, but with a fever that seemed to take root in his mind as well as his body. Sival sent to the city for a healer, and one came to examine Yuda. Yuste was not allowed into the room while the healer, a shamanka, was there, but Sival told her about it afterwards.

'In the olden days, there were times when someone became a shaman after a serious illness, whether of the body or the mind,' he said. 'This isn't the same, but it is a kind of metamorphosis. You must have noticed that Yuda's power signature has changed colour.'

'Will mine change like that?' said Yuste.

'Zyon! I hope not,' said Sival, using the one expletive their mother was willing to allow. 'I think the trauma of the attack has triggered the change. My Masters in Inde taught me that, while girls gain their powers in a slow but steady onset, boys can find theirs increase in a sudden jump. Girls undoubtedly have the advantage; they have more time to learn how to use their powers before they need to.'

Yuste peeped in at her brother, lying in his bed. They were not sharing a room while he was ill; he suffered from fearsome dreams and sometimes woke screaming, crying that the burning Olivier was coming after him. When Yuste shut her eyes, she could see her brother's durmat, silver and blue; in time, the blue would fade.

The fight with Olivier and the events that preceded it had driven all thought of Savorin out of her head – and her dreams. Sometimes she dreamed of Aude, and her pale skin just seen through the water, her soft mouth and her loose, wet hair; then she remembered her brother shouting at her, the anger and hate in his eyes, because they both wanted the same thing; the same girl.

She had talked to Sival about this quarrel. Even though he was a man, she found him easier to confide in than her mother. He never seemed to judge her; he listened, and told her what he thought, as if she was an adult. He was unable to advise much; he pointed out that Aude had shown no interest in either of them, except as friends. She was closer to Yuste because they were both girls, and liked each other's company.

'But what she may feel for you beyond that?' Sival shrugged. It was impossible to know.

Yuste knew in her heart it was too soon to think about such things. She loved Aude in the same way she loved her brother; desire did not enter into it. But she had not forgotten the dream she had shared with him, and wondered which of them had dreamed it first.

Meanwhile, Yuda was absent. He was either delirious, shouting out and crying with fear; or deeply asleep, lost in some distant world where they could not reach him. They took turns sitting by his bedside, even Reb Mordechai, who read to him, not from religious books, but the old stories that Yuda had loved when he was small, concerning the wizard mice and their adventures in Aravi.

When her turn came, Yuste told her brother everything that had happened at school that day. She did not try to share her thoughts with him, because Sival had warned her that, in his distress, Yuda might drag her down into whatever darkness he had entered.

'You're too close,' he said. 'When he returns, he will be happy to see you.'

'But what if he doesn't come back?' said Yuste.

Sival shook his head. 'He will come back,' he said. 'I've seen this happen in Inde. And this is Yuda, Yuste. He is like you; he is tough. You have survived illnesses that would have killed weaker children. Shamans are not like the rest of us; you have to be strong to withstand the power. And now you've seen what it can do, set free.'

'It shouldn't have happened,' said Yuste, balling her fists.

'Indeed not. Someone should have stopped Olivier Baudoin sooner, not least his father. If they had done, he might be alive today. But in picking on your brother, he chose the wrong victim.'

On the day Yuda returned from his long absence, Yuste was sitting at his bedside, holding his hand in hers. She was not thinking about much, when she looked up to find his eyes were open, black and clear.

'There is One in Zyon,' he said in a weak voice.

'One, and one only,' said Yuste. She couldn't stop herself; she bent over him and kissed him on the cheek. Her brother lay motionless, gazing at her. He looked pale, the colour of ivory, and his eyes seemed huge, like the eyes of a young animal. Yuste studied him and understood that she had lost her little brother. This was not yet a man, or even a youth; but the Yuda who had returned was not the same as the one who had gone away. Something had changed in him.

'Have I been gone long?' he said. He seemed shy of her; he pulled the covers up to his chin.

Yuste sat staring at him. In spite of everything, she was so happy he had come back. She had not quite been able to believe Sival's promise that he would return.

'Nearly six weeks,' she said. 'You've missed a whole school term.'

'I must have been very ill,' he said, glancing out of the window. 'Did they make you sleep somewhere else?'

'I took Sival's room in the attic, and he either sat up with you, or slept downstairs on the couch. Someone was always with you, all day and all night.'

Yuda looked at his hands, which were resting on the coverlet. The left one was still bandaged.

'Am I in trouble?' he said.

'No. There was an inquest, and you were exonerated. Everyone agreed that it was self-defence. But *Tateh* wants to send you away to the Yeshiva in Masalyar as soon as you are well. He thinks you will be safer there.'

Yuda shut his eyes. His face looked drawn.

'It's too late,' he said. 'I have killed a man. And my powers are free. I have to be a shaman now, whether I want to or not. I have to make amends for the death I caused. I need to be a healer, as soon as I'm old enough to learn. I can't go back to the way things were.'

Yuste smoothed his hair. She was sorry, but also relieved.

'I think I knew that,' she said. 'When can we *sprechen*?'

'Soon. I need to think about where I've been. And I must talk to Sival.'

'*Mameh* will want to see you too.'

Yuda covered his eyes with his hand. 'Not just yet, Yustka,' he said. 'I'd like it to be just the two of us for a bit. If you don't mind.'

'Of course I don't mind! I've missed you so much. I was afraid you wouldn't return,' said Yuste.

Yuda's good hand stole out, and took hold of hers. His grip felt stronger than before.

'I kept seeing him on fire,' he said. 'Again and again.'

Yuste saw tears at the corners of his eyes. She felt terribly sad; she had no idea how to comfort him.

'I know,' she said. 'You talked in your sleep. Some of it wasn't good.'

'I can still hear him screaming,' said Yuda. He shook his head. 'I thought I would go mad. But...'

He paused for a long time, staring into space. Yuste began to think he must have lost consciousness again, but she waited and did not try to waken him.

'After a while, it stopped,' said her brother, rolling his head on the pillow so he could look at her. 'And I found myself back outside the walls of Savorin.'

It was such a long time since anyone had mentioned the sunken city that Yuste started. Her brother squeezed her hand, as if he was the one comforting her.

'I was by myself, this time,' he said. 'I felt as if it was a test I had to pass.'

'What happened?' she said, feeling intensely curious.

'I'm not sure.' His eyes stopped focusing on her, as if he was looking at something far away, just out of reach. 'There is something down there, Yuste. I followed the wall as far as I could go, with my right hand on the stones. And in the end, I came to a door. It was partly blocked by rubble, sand and weed, but I managed to clear some away. There was a rush of water from inside, as if I'd taken the stopper out of a bottle. And as the silt began to settle, I found that I'd opened a gap, just large enough for me to peep through.'

He stopped, and gave a quick shiver.

'What did you see?' said Yuste.

Yuda's eyes fixed on her once more, returning to the present. 'I'm not sure,' he said. 'The water inside was turbid, but it looked like a chamber. There may have been glints of metal. And something pale, like bone. I didn't like it. I felt as if someone was watching me, from deep inside the room.'

'Do you think it was that white person we saw – the day I woke the storm?'

They gazed into each other's eyes, as serious as adults. They sensed this was something they would have to deal with by themselves, without help from their parents or Sival, just as Yuda had fought his first battle alone.

'I don't know,' he said. 'I wondered if it would try to catch me. Or lure me inside.'

'Was that all of your Journey?' said Yuste, using the word in the sense Sival had taught them.

'No. I don't think I understand the other things that happened. I'm not sure I could even describe them. I feel rather as if I – what's the word for when a frog changes into a tadpole?'

'Metamorphosed,' said Yuste, solemnly. 'But you don't look different.'

'Zyon, I hope not!'

To his sister's mixed amusement and dismay, he threw the covers aside and sprang out of bed, intending to go and look in a mirror. His legs were too weak to bear his weight, and he dropped to the floor, lying there with a surprised expression, stark naked. Yuste snatched up the coverlet and threw it over him, noticing that he looked skinnier than ever – but could he have grown taller? She left him lying on the floor and ran out on the landing to call Sival, who she knew was not far away, working at the desk in his room now she had vacated it for the day.

The Teacher came springing down the stairs from the attic, and his surprise matched that of Yuda lying on the floor so much that Yuste giggled.

'My legs don't work, Guru-ji!' said Yuda, as Sival scooped him up and dumped him on the bed.

'My poor spine,' said Sival, sitting in the chair where Yuste had sat, and rubbing the small of his back. 'I'm glad to see you have rejoined us, *mon enfant*. Where have you been?'

'I'm not sure. I went on a Journey. I was trying to tell Yuste. We think I may have metamorphosed.'

He looked so worried that Sival had to smile in his turn. 'You don't look too different,' he said. 'But your durmat has changed. I would expect that. In the old days, one of the first signs of becoming a shaman was falling gravely ill. In your case, extreme danger overcame the block I had put on your powers. You needed them in order to stay alive. But sadly for one so young, you have also learnt that there is always a price when you take a life.'

Yuda lifted his bandaged hand and examined it. 'I thought it would be different. I mean, I never intended to kill him. I just wanted to make him go away.'

'That is why I put the block on your powers in the first place. But these things cannot be maintained for ever. Now more than ever, you need to learn how to use and control your powers.'

'*Tateh* wants me to go to the Yeshiva in Masalyar,' said Yuda, lowering his hand and gazing at Sival.

Sival nodded. 'I know. Your mother and I have tried to dissuade him. For different reasons, neither of us thinks you should be sent to religion school. You are not cut out to be a scribe or Rashim, vocations that require considerable diligence and fondness for study. Your father, like many a Wanderer before him, would love his son to become a holy man. His own parents were merchants in the port of Ades. He emigrated to Lefranu to train as a physician. And now... he wants his son to do what he would love to have done. This is common with parents. They want to give their sons – and daughters – all the opportunities they missed. Sometimes the child's wishes are in perfect agreement with those of the parents. But this is more than a matter of duty, *mes enfants*. Fathers must recognise that their sons are separate people. And shamans are wholly different. Your mother has always grasped this, but Reb Mordechai has not.'

Yuda turned his head away, but Yuste knew he was weeping. She wept too.

'I'm already a disappointment to him,' Yuda said. 'How am I going to tell him I can't do it?'

Sival sat without answering for a while, with his chin tucked into his chest. As was often the case with the Teshvet, Yuste had no idea what he was thinking.

'You need to give yourself time. And we will talk to him. I think he may already know in his heart that that bird has flown.'

Yuste went downstairs to fetch her mother, and watched with a slight pang that was not exactly envy as the small woman sprang up the stairs, calling her son's name. Soon after, Sival descended the staircase to find her standing at the foot with her hand on the newel post, gazing up into the dark.

'Let's go out for a walk, Yuste,' he said.

They strolled up to the headland near the twin's den, where they could gaze out to sea. And once again, Yuste felt the sense that Savorin was calling out to her, like a yearning. She had never felt it more strongly than today.

'Can you hear singing?' she said.

Sival listened to the wind, and shook his head. 'I can hear seabirds. But no singing. Sometimes one can imagine that there are voices in the wind.'

'If someone jumped off the cliff here, would they survive?'

Sival gave a wry smile. 'I hope you are not planning to test that possibility, Yuste. There is no chance they would survive. It is the kind of place where you have to be a vigilant in foggy weather. I don't think it is popular with suicides. Not many people come this way, unless they are visiting your father or mother.'

'I miss Aude. We haven't met since term ended. And I can't go round to her house because her father abominates Wanderers.'

'I suspect he is more worried about his daughter consorting with shamans,' said Sival. 'They are an unusual family. Though I have only met Madame d'Iforas, Aude and Thibault, they seem to be somehow – medieval. I don't think the local people know what to make of them. I'm sure it would do no harm to send Aude a message that your brother has reawakened. You could take a letter to the post in the main village.'

In the end, Yuste wrote and sealed four letters, one each to Aude, Cricri, François and Gustave. She summoned the gang to meet her at the sea cave on the day after Kingsday, when Wanderers would do no work. There was a special meal and any girl children would play the part of the Kingsday Bride, who represented the Shkine, the female form of the One descending to Earth. This Kingsday would be a special celebration because it was the first time Yuda had been able to join his family at the table. Sival always ate with them, since he was the household's honoured guest, and he could help with any tasks they were forbidden to do because of the holy feast.

Yuste decided to arrange the meeting for the evening after Kingsday went out. The days were getting longer, and the sun did not set till after eight, so it gave them plenty of time. She did not tell her brother what she had planned until the Kingsday meal had finished. He was up and dressed, but still shaky on his feet; he looked less gaunt and uncertain, more like his old self.

They walked down to the bay by one of the less steep paths that followed the track of a narrow stream that emptied into the bay. Yuste led the way, with Yuda behind her, leaning on a walking stick their mother had borrowed from someone in the village.

The twins did not talk out loud, but they were used to sharing overlapping thoughts that were not fully voiced. Some were fragments of words and images; they had communicated like this long before they had learned to speak. They used a mixture of Franj, Sklavan and the Wanderer tongue, which anyone who did not know all three languages would have found incomprehensible. Occasionally they would punctuate their silent conversation with gestures, like a form of sign language. They knew no-one else could overhear what they were saying, and it was a useful knack, especially as their parents were more over-protective than ever.

– *You didn't ask Thibault?*

– *I told Aude she could bring him if she wanted. He's okay. But I really wanted it to be just us.*

Yuda did not answer; he understood. She had sketched out her thoughts to him, in just enough detail for him to know what she was planning to do. She was unsure whether he approved; he seemed to have developed a greater reserve since wakening from his trance, and he was better at warding his thoughts. She knew he wanted to protect her from any flashbacks to the moment of horror after he set Olivier Baudoin on fire. He did not want her to share them, and he was reluctant to reveal what he had seen in the underworld.

When they had clambered up the rocks to the sea cave, they were relieved to find the others waiting for them; Aude had not brought Thibault, though she had let him know where she was going. The three boys jumped up and hugged Yuda, kissing him on both cheeks, according to local custom. Aude did so as well, producing such a reaction of mixed dismay and pleasure from Yuda that Yuste struggled not to laugh.

She was startled to see how delighted the boys were with Yuda's crime.

'You did it! You killed Olivier Baudoin at last,' said Cricri, hugging Yuda.

'I never meant to kill him...' said Yuda, looking uncomfortable.

'He had it coming,' said Gustave, saying more in Yuste's hearing than he had done in a long while. 'Everybody knew he tried to rape you. He was disgusting. And now they'll never bother you again.'

'I'm not so sure,' said François. 'They might try to wind him up and make him do it again. I mean, most people round here have never seen a shaman at work!'

'It's not good if people are scared of you. And lots of people believe that Wanderers do magic anyway,' said Yuda, making a face.

They sat down round the small fire that had been kindled in the centre of the cave. There were potatoes dug into the ash beneath the fire, cooking slowly; and someone had brought a tripod with a coffee pot to hang over the flames. As the sun went down, the light from the fire was welcome, and the children lit several lanterns with stubs of candle.

Yuste sat next to Aude, who had brought some knitting to keep her hands occupied, and they chatted about nothing in particular for a while. It was important not to think too much about what lay ahead, which Yuste had outlined in her letter.

The boys were playing cards. Cricri had a well-thumbed pack that was one of the few things left by his father. There were a few cards missing, which made some games difficult to play. Yuste looked at the firelight umbering their faces; umber was a reddish brown pigment that was labelled in the paint-box her mother had bought her from Masalyar. She thought how comfortable and at ease the boys looked together; Cricri sitting cross-legged, Francois lounging by the fire, Yuda sitting on his heels, and Gustave somewhat awkwardly with his knees drawn up beneath his chin. Occasionally one of them would swear or laugh, depending on whether he had won or lost a hand.

Yuste reflected that these were not the type of companions her father would have wanted for Yuda. He had longed for his son to become a yeshiva *bokher* like other Wanderer boys – respectable boys, whose fathers lived in Masalyar, and attended the Beit every Kingsday. But it was too late, and had been for years. Reb Mordechai had chosen to live miles from the city, where his children had grown up surrounded by Dzuzukim. And the other boys treated Yuda as one of them; they were all outsiders, and they had found a way to rub along together, regardless of whether their parents approved.

'What are you thinking, Yuste?' said Aude, leaning against her. Her skin soft and warm, her hair smelling slightly of vanilla. Yuste sighed. She wondered about trying to kiss Aude, the way Yuda had done, but could not imagine it happening. She did not even know what the word was for women who loved other women. She knew that Wanderer Law forbade men to love men.

'It must be nearly time,' she said out loud.

They were waiting for the moon to rise. And when the moon rose, they would have to leave the comfort and safety of the cave, and go down to the beach. They had a job to do, and they had not told anyone about it, apart from Thibault.

'Has anyone got a watch?' said Yuda.

François held up a pocket watch on a chain he had borrowed from his father, without asking. The boys inspected it and discovered that the time was after midnight. The task they needed to do could not be done in daylight; though the sunken city of Savorin only existed after dark, it would be too dangerous to go near it without the light of the moon.

Yuste stood up and went to the edge of the cave. The moon was rising over the sea; it was a gibbous moon, not fully round. She turned and looked back at the boys, feeling a pang near her heart as she wondered whether she would see them here like this again; but then Aude came to stand beside her, and slipped her arm round Yuste's waist, and her heart leapt instead. She found the other girl's sea-green eyes looking into hers with what seemed like a wisdom older than her years.

'I think you're right, Yuste,' said Aude. 'We can't leave it there.'

Yuda came to stand on the other side of Yuste, peering out at the sky. He was wearing a hat with a dented crown and a brim like a Wanderer man; a little gentleman, Yuste thought.

'We'd better go,' he said to his sister. Yuste could tell he was scared and trying not to show it. There was a dewdrop on the end of his nose, and he hastily blew into a handkerchief.

One by one, they climbed down to the sand below. The moon was bright enough to cast their shadows on the ground, and both Yuda and Yuste could see well in the dark, like cats. They formed a small procession down to the shore, where Cricri had left his rowing boat, with the oars shipped. He was the only member of the gang who lived in the *port de pêche*, the part of the village that bordered the sea. Calling it a port was a bit grandiose, but the seaside at Sankt Eglis was more important than the landward part where the Mayor and the local bourgeois lived.

One by one, they clambered into the skiff. Yuste took the tiller, since that was her role when she and Yuda went out in their craft. Aude sat beside her, trailing her hand in the water, and stirring up trails of luminescence. Cricri took charge of the main pair of oars, since it was his boat; Gustave took the second pair. Yuda sat in the prow with the lantern, and François by him. It was a boat built to carry adults rather than children, or Gustave's weight would have made it sit too low in the water.

Yuda delayed them by fiddling with matches to light the lantern.

'Can't you use your powers?' said Cricri.

'I can't use them for something like that!' croaked Yuda, in a weird voice that seemed to be deep and high-pitched at the same time.

'He's gone,' said François, and the other boys fell about laughing.

'Zyon,' said Yuda, feeling his larynx.

'Now you know what it's like,' said Gustave, whose voice had broken some months previously.

Once the lantern was lit, Cricri dipped the oars in the water and rowed the boat away from the shore, with Yuste steering. They all knew where they were heading; there was a buoy anchored close to the site of Savorin, to warn passing shipping of the rocks nearby, which some said were all that remained of the church spires.

The plan had been agreed beforehand. They would row out to the buoy and drop anchor nearby, in the lee of the cliff where Yuda and Yuste's house stood. Gustave and François would stay in the boat while the others dived down to the city they had seen in their dreams.

66

But if they found the wall, what then? They could hold their breath for a long time, but it might not be long enough. François had said they would need a bathyscaphe or diving bell to be able to explore the sea bed; and things like that would only be found in Masalyar.

'There's a thing called a shaman door,' said Yuda. 'Sometimes, you can pass through them. It's like the entrance into another world or dimension.'

'It's no good if you and Yuste can enter but Aude and Cricri can't,' said François. 'How will we know that you haven't just drowned?'

'I don't think you need to be a shaman to use a shaman door,' said Yuste. 'It is real. A portal. Teshvet can't see it, but they can pass through.'

'We'll send you a signal,' said Yuda. 'Yuste or I will send up a flare, using our powers.'

'Can you even do that?' said François. He was older than the others, and they respected his opinions, and his caution.

'Yuste can,' said Aude, remembering that first meeting on the beach.

They stripped down, the boys to their drawers and the girls to their chemises and bloomers. Yuste wondered about the propriety of being so thinly dressed, but it was no time to worry about the rules of modesty. There was a certain amount of shivering and embarrassment, since both Cricri and Yuda were knock-kneed and pigeon-chested. But it was time to go; one by one, they took the plunge over the edge of the boat, slipping into the water like seals off a rock. And they dived into the gloom below, where the sea itself seemed darker than night.

***

Aude was the last of the divers. Cricri and the twins seemed to plunge downwards like shooting stars, leaving a wake of luminescence behind them. The water was turbid and dark, and she feared losing sight of them. She followed Yuste's pale feet, wishing she had not volunteered to go. The only sound she could hear was the water in her ears and the pulse of her blood; any danger would come upon her unawares, when she was deaf and could hardly see.

They seemed to be descending a long way. Though Aude had practised holding her breath, she did not know how long she could keep it in. She wondered whether Yuda knew what he was looking for. She wished Yuste had taken the lead; Yuste was the one whose instincts Aude trusted.

With a shower of bubbles, Yuda came surging out of the depths like an otter, seized her hand and pulled her after him. Aude had no choice but to go; she was glad when Yuste caught her other hand, and she glimpsed Cricri on the other side. She feared her head would burst and her lungs explode, when Yuste pulled her close and blew air into her mouth – air she could breathe! She almost forgot to close her mouth in astonishment and glimpsed Yuste's face smiling at her though the bubbles. Did shamans have gills? Yuda did the same for Cricri soon after. And Aude felt as if she had turned into a fish, or an amphibian like a frog; the air they had given her seemed to last.

The four of them had reached the sea floor. And there was the wall Aude had seen in her dreams, though it seemed much darker and coated in weed and moss. It might not be a wall at all, but an outcrop of stone that had been uncovered and eroded by the action of the water.

Yuda released her hand, and she saw his pale shape, kicking through the water towards the wall, and stretching out to touch it. In her mind, there was a flash of light, as if someone had opened a door. She blinked, and Yuda was still there, running his hands over the stones of the wall. And she saw it; blocks of ashlar that had edges, shaped by tools. Yuda glanced back towards the three of them, bubbles trailing from his lips; she thought he smiled. And he gave them the thumbs up; he had found his shaman door.

Yuste lifted her hand over head, and fired off the flare as she had promised. Aude saw the water shiver as the blue spark travelled up towards the surface; she wondered why the water did not put it out. She and the others swam closer to Yuda, who was standing with one hand on the wall. He stretched out his hand towards Aude with a gesture of impatience, there was another flash of light – and she found herself falling forward through a door, what looked like an ordinary front door on one of the village houses – into a dry room where there was air, daylight – and no sea.

**

The children found themselves in a fine room, with champagne-coloured carpet on the floor, mirrors on the walls, and crystal chandeliers suspended from the ceiling. They were dripping wet and under-dressed for the occasion. The room was empty apart from them, and they looked round in awe at the richness of everything. The couches were covered in shot gold silk, the walls between the mirrors were sheathed in striped wood veneer, and everywhere the children saw crisp geometric details; black piping on the bolster cushions, zebra-skin rugs on the floor, and ornate glass lamps set into the walls.

'I'm not sure we should be here,' said Yuste, voicing what they were all thinking.

'Is this really what's under the sea? Is this Savorin?' said Cricri.

'I don't know,' said Yuda. 'This isn't what I saw in my dreams. I saw a ruined castle, filled with treasure.'

'I suppose this is a sort of treasure,' said Aude. She moved to the far side of the room, where a grand piano stood, its wooden case so polished and varnished that she could see her face reflected in the surface. The others came to join her; they had never seen anything like it. There were other instruments perched on tables surrounding the piano: a portable harp made from gilded wood, a lute, and a vyel, an instrument that Yuste and Yuda were learning to play.

'It's almost as if they were left here to tempt us,' said Yuste, as Aude's hand strayed out to touch the golden harp. She had not touched one since she left the castle, and she felt an ache, a longing to pick up the unknown instrument and test its strings.

'Maybe it's a test,' said Yuda. 'But are we meant to leave the instruments alone, or play them?'

Cricri stroked the lid of the piano as if it was a large animal such as a horse or a cow. He smiled wistfully. 'I don't think any of us even knows how to play this one,' he said. 'I'd love to hear it, just once.'

'Someone must live here,' said Aude, lifting her head to look at the white ceiling and the hanging crystal chandeliers with their electric ampoules, something she had encountered only recently.

'I'm not sure 'live' is the word I'd use,' said Yuda, frowning. 'It feels wrong to me.'

'And me,' said Yuste. 'But we came here for a purpose. To exorcise Savorin. To put the ghosts to sleep.'

An inner door opened, and they all jumped. A tall woman appeared, with hair so fair it was white, set with a circlet of pearls. She wore a beaded dress that hung no lower than her knees, made from silk, lace and droplets of glass; it swung as she walked, clinging to her body. Her stockings were made of translucent silk, and on her feet were black velvet pumps with vertiginous heels. She was smoking a cigarette in a long, ebony holder.

'Darling,' she said to someone unseen in the room she had just left. 'It's four children. How simply marvellous!'

69

She was joined by a man in a shiny black suit, with huge padded shoulders and baggy trousers. His hair was slicked back with pomade that gave it the appearance of oil. Like the woman, he was tall, and as pale as her pearl necklace. Or as pale as bone, thought Aude. She was conscious that the Vasilyevich twins were bristling like a pair of cats; they looked wide-eyed and frightened, as if sensing something bad. She glanced at Cricri, who was Teshvet, like her, and saw that he too looked troubled.

'What have we here?' said the man, swaggering across the carpet to inspect them. He did not seem ghostly; Aude noticed his manicured fingers, playing with a stubby, oblong metal box. She found out what it was for when he flipped the lid open, made a flame, and lit a cigarette he had dangling from his mouth.

'Who are you?' said Yuda. Aude realised his teeth were chattering, though she did not know whether from cold or fright.

'Later,' said the woman, reclining on one of the silk-upholstered couches. 'You must be frozen. Why don't you go and get changed? Then we can offer you something to eat, and after that we can talk.'

'Is this Savorin?' said Cricri. 'We didn't know it would look like this. I thought it would be abandoned palaces, dead bones, and cursed treasure.'

'Come here, little blackamoor,' said the woman, turning towards him. Her lips were dark red, painted in a perfect cupid's bow. 'How splendid a page you would make, dressed in silks and satins. Wouldn't that be a fine thing, to stay here with me, away from poverty and want? Your dark skin would set off my pale complexion so prettily. You would be the foil to my beauty.'

Cricri drew himself up. 'That's very nice of you, Madame, but I can't leave my mother,' he said. 'Since father abandoned us, I'm all she's got.'

'Perhaps your father intended to come back, but he was drowned. And his bones lie on the floor of some far away sea,' said the woman.

'You don't know that!' shouted Cricri. Yuda laid his hand on the other boy's arm.

'Cricri isn't a toy,' he said. 'And anyway, *Mameh* has told us not to accept food from strangers. We don't know anything about you. We didn't know any of this was here. And this is a shaman world. My sister and I are shamans.'

'Did you hear that, Maurice?' said the woman, stretching out her long neck so her head fell back. She laughed heartily. 'A shaman-world! How quaint. I have never heard it called that before. And these strange creatures are shamans. They look so starved and pale. Why don't you sit down, *kindeleh*? There's no need to be formal. You are among friends.'

Maurice circled the four children, inspecting them. Aude thought he seemed nervous, which was an odd reaction. She wondered what he was afraid of.

'I'm not sure, old thing,' he said to the woman. 'They seem frightfully grubby. Do you really want them sitting on your Biedermeier sofas? For one thing, they're wringing wet. They may stain the upholstery.'

'You're such a bore, Maurice,' said the woman, pouting. 'Go and fix me another drink. And while you're about it, summon the servants to make cocoa for the children. I shouldn't think they'll be interested in a Gin and It.'

Maurice turned on his heel and stalked across the parquet floor in his spotless black leather shoes, which squeaked as he walked.

'Why did you call us *'kindeleh'*?' said Yuste. 'That's a Wanderer word.'

'I know all about you, Darling,' said the woman. 'I've been interested in you for a long time. Why don't you come and sit here beside me? And bring your friend. What's her name? *Aude. Aude D'Iforas.*'

Aude shivered. She found the woman's eyes looking at her over the edge of her glass, knowing and unkind.

'How do you know my name?' she said.

The woman blew smoke between her ruby-red lips. 'Darling, I never forget a name – or a face. And you three – it was you, I am sure – were the ones who called me back. You might as well have spoken my name.'

'We never summoned you!' shouted Yuda. 'We didn't summon anybody!'

The woman did not answer at once; she gave Yuda a long, cool stare, until he went red and had to look away.

'I think you did,' she said. 'Time forward and time backward. Aude came swimming to meet you. The girl from the sea. She has always been there; always waiting to meet you. The sweet scent, like the perfume of beeswax; hanging in the air, stronger than roses in summer. And the light!' She laughed. 'It was so heady. One could almost become intoxicated with it.'

Aude had no idea what she was talking about, and she saw from Yuda and Yuste's faces that they were equally puzzled.

'Are you saying that was you?' said Yuda. 'The white figure with the skull face?'

'It was a figure of speech,' said the woman. 'You saw what you imagined – and feared – would lie in the deep. If Savorin returned, surely it would come as ranks of dead horsemen riding the waves into the land and swallowing it up?'

Yuda sat down on the couch opposite the woman as if his knees had given way, and the others sat beside him, too tired and scared to worry about whether they were going to stain the upholstery. The woman smiled at them indulgently.

'That's better,' she said. 'Though Maurice seems to be taking a long time to make me a drink. I expect he's trying to explain the concept of cocoa to the staff.'

'We really shouldn't impose on you,' said Yuste, imitating her mother. 'And our teacher warned us not to accept food or drink in the underworld. Even if it isn't deadly, it usually comes with – obligations.'

'What a clever student you are, Yuste Vasilyevich,' said the woman. 'I wonder whether you would like me to foretell your future?'

Yuste looked at her lap. 'I'm not sure you can do that,' she said. 'Only the One knows the future, because he is beyond time and space.'

'Are you a fortune-teller?' said Cricri. 'There was an old gypsy woman at the travelling fair, but she told everyone pretty much the same thing. I expect you'll tell Yuste something nasty to frighten her. Even if it's not true.'

'I could tell your fortune, Cricri son of Adamah. You see, I know your father's name.'

Cricri sat back, his eyes wide with shock. Then he burst into tears, and Yuste put her arm round his shoulders. Yuda jumped up.

'I think you're cruel,' he said. 'Maybe you do know what will happen to my sister, and the rest of us. But it doesn't give you the right to frighten us.'

'Poor Yuda,' said the woman. She shook her head. 'How little you know. And yet you have killed your first man, before you are a man yourself. Remember how that went?'

She snapped her fingers, and the figure of Olivier Baudoin appeared in the space between the couches, a faceless, howling thing on fire that staggered towards them from an infinite distance. Yuda

72

cried out, and hid his face in his hands, but Yuste jumped up and stretched out her left arm; she shouted words Aude did not understand, ancient words that conjured a row of dancing golden characters in the air between them and the figure, like the ones Yuda had used weeks ago to protect them against the threat from the sea. As Aude watched, the phantom dissolved into air, leaving no trace, not even a smear of ash on the carpet.

Yuste wrapped her arms round her brother and hugged him. Aude felt drawn to them, and she put her arms round them both; she could feel Yuda shaking with sobs, and Yuste rocking him as if he was a child.

'I hate you,' Yuste said to the woman, who was watching them coolly, with a faint smile on her lips.

'So you have the power of the Wanderers,' she said.

'I don't. Wanderers aren't magical.'

The woman shrugged. 'Not all of them. They're Teshvet like the rest. But you just did something... I'm not sure you even know what you did.'

'I recited a Blessing against evil. And you know that wasn't Olivier Baudoin's ghost. It was an illusion, like a fetch. I don't know who you are, but you can't be that powerful or you wouldn't be trapped here.'

'But I am no longer trapped, Yuste daughter of Kaila. You have set me free. And now I am free, you must decide what to do about me.'

Hearing those words, Aude shuddered. They reminded her of the magic she and her friend had been trying to perform. And they too had set something free. She stared fearfully at the woman's face, but saw no trace of recognition. This had nothing to do with her conjuration; this was a spirit from the deep, and one more powerful than any of them could have imagined. Male or female, it could be either, or neither; it had chosen a useful shape to appear to them.

Yuste released her brother, who was calmer, and went to the woman, seated on the couch. She stood in front of her, a small, untidy figure with damp clothes and hair. Her wet plaits looked like rat's tails.

'I want you to go back to sleep,' she said. 'I never meant to waken you in the first place.'

'Oh yes you did. You fired out to sea with anger in your heart. And I came in answer to your anger.'

Yuste did not reply; she stood with her hands clasped in front of her. Aude detected that Yuda was alert, watching and listening to his sister. She wondered what it must be like to hear someone else's thoughts, all the time; you would never feel alone, but you would never be private. She stroked his back, and he shivered, as if he had not noticed she was holding him. Aude thought he and Yuste were communicating, though she could not detect what they were thinking; they both had an intent look, as if they were looking inward rather than outward.

Cricri touched her arm. Aude jumped, and she saw him smiling and holding his finger to his lips. The white-haired woman was staring at Yuste, holding her gaze like a cobra hypnotizing its prey. Cricri took her hand in his, and drew her away, towards the tables where the silent instruments lay. Aude squeezed his hand in return, making him look at her. She dared not whisper, but she hoped he could tell from her expression that she hesitated to do what he asked. Cricri nodded at her, and before she could stop him, he had picked up the golden harp – the most beautiful of the instruments and the only one she knew how to play – and placed it in her arms.

The harp screamed. The pillar was carved with a woman's face, which screeched like a harpy. It was all Aude could do not to drop the instrument on the floor. The silver-haired woman sprang to her feet.

'So!' she said. 'Little thieves.'

Behind her, Aude saw Yuste crumple to the floor, as if she had been held up by an invisible cord. Yuda hurried to her, and tried to lift her.

'We are not thieves,' said Cricri. 'We wanted to see what happened when we played the instruments – ah...'

The woman flicked her cigarette holder, now empty, upwards, and the boy was dragged off his feet and hurled into the air where he remained, dangling close to the ceiling, his eyes wide open and his mouth gaping in silent cry of pain.

'Please stop! Please let him go,' said Aude. 'I'll do anything you want.'

'Anything?' said the woman. She snapped her fingers and Cricri, like Yuste, fell to the floor and lay unmoving in a heap. Aude could not see whether he was breathing.

'Yes,' said Aude. She tried not to think what that might mean; what the woman might ask of her.

'Sit down beside me and play,' said the woman. She sat on the couch once more, and patted the silken seat next to her.

'What about the others?' said Aude.

'You said you would do anything I wanted, Aude daughter of Gaudry. Leave them.'

Aude glanced at Cricri as she passed; he lay still, his head tucked in, like a bundle of clothes. She could not bear to think he might be dead; she could not imagine telling his mother what had happened. Yuste and Yuda were huddled together, and Yuste appeared lost in a trance; her eyes were turned up in her head. Yuda glared at Aude from under his hair, a wild, frightened look; and she knew that, whatever she needed to do, she must not fail.

The couch was soft and comfortable to sit on. Seen from up close, the woman's beauty seemed flawless; there were no cracks in her make-up, and she looked young and fresh, like a flower before the sun had touched it.

'What do you want me to sing, my lady?' Aude said. She was careful to speak with downcast eyes, as if to one of her betters.

'I'm sure you know many songs, Aude d'Iforas. Put your hands to the strings, and sing me the first song in your heart.'

Aude closed her eyes. There was a song: *À la claire fontaine*, the one her mother loved.

À la claire fontaine m'en allant promener
J'ai trouvé l'eau si belle que je m'y suis baignée.
Il y a longtemps que je t'aime, jamais je ne t'oublierai

It was a song about lost love, or lost friendship; a young girl left by her lover.

As I was walking by the clear fountain,
I found the water so lovely I had to bathe.
I've loved you for so long, I will never forget you

As Aude sang, and there were more verses, she became lost in the music and sadness of the song. It seemed to echo through her, and she wondered why it drew her; because she had lost her friend and her former home? She felt her lungs filling with air, and her mouth with music; the tune seemed to end too soon.

'A love song!' said the woman. 'And who will you love, *la Belle Aude?*'

Aude felt her cheeks redden. With her pale skin and red hair, blushing was all too obvious. She felt anything but *belle*. And she knew the woman was mocking her.

'Is that what you wanted?' she said, taking care not to look the woman in the eye.

'Oh, I want more than that. I think you know what I want, Aude. A promise.'

Aude shivered. She had to look up into the woman's eyes at last. And they seemed to be hollow, black pits into which she fell, a long way down, much further than under the sea.

A promise. It was as simple as that. One life, to let the others go. She had thought of keeping Cricri with her, but she would be satisfied with Aude.

'No,' said Aude. 'You can't do that.' She shook her head.

The woman slipped her hand under Aude's chin, forcing her to look up again into her eyes.

'Not yet,' she said. 'But I will wait. You will come to me in the end, of your own free will.'

'What do you mean?' said Aude. Tears blinded her, and she saw only a dazzling pattern of light from the lamps, and the black holes in the woman's face.

'How long – how lonely – how hungry,' said the woman in a dreamy voice. 'I have been here many centuries. More than you could imagine.'

'What about your... husband?' said Aude, thinking about the man in the black suit. He had been gone a long time.

'Oh. Him.' The woman pursed her lips. Her eyes became human again. 'Let's say I have servants, but they are not human. They lack the warmth of human blood, and a human heartbeat.'

Aude shivered. She wrapped her arms round the harp, as if it could protect her. And she noticed that the face had returned to perfect stillness, a carved mask made from gilded wood, as if it had never cried out in rage and fear.

'So if I agree to that, you'll let us go,' she said.

Aude became aware that Yuste and Yuda had risen to their feet and were standing nearby, watching and listening. She wondered how much they had heard.

'Agree to what?' said Yuda. 'What have you said to her?'

The woman glanced at the twins. 'You should know better than to interrupt,' she said, coldly.

Yuda glowered back at her. 'I want to know what she's agreed to. And what have you done to Cricri?'

The woman shook her head. She lifted a clutch bag studded with pearls – real pearls? – from the seat behind her, and drew out a fresh cigarette to fit into her holder.

'I could keep you all here,' she said, addressing Yuda. 'No-one would find you. They would think you lost at sea. And you could stay here with me, living like princes – and princesses – and never needing to grow up. You can see what a fine place this is. You would lack nothing. Food, drink fine clothes, music – and safety. Nothing to fear, ever again.'

Yuste laid her hand on her brother's shoulder. 'We'd be dead,' she said. 'You need to feed off our blood, spilled in the water. And if you took the four of us, you could last a long time. Hundreds of years.'

'What a pity,' said the woman. 'So clever, but not so pretty. And how much you love your twin. What will you do when he grows up? He's already restless. One small fishing village, son of the village doctor, is too small for him.'

'That's not fair,' said Yuda. 'You don't know what will happen to us. I don't think you have that kind of power. You're not a goddess. And my sister is clever. If I go, I'll take her with me.'

'My offer stands,' said the woman.

Behind her, Aude saw that Cricri had risen to his feet. His face looked grey in the weird light, but he was alive. He was holding something in his hands. Before Aude could tell what it was, he raised it high and brought it down with all his force on the woman's head.

And her head split open...

What emerged was smooth and blunt, like the head of a snake, but grey as a worm. It slithered out of the body, which it sloughed off like discarded skin, uncoiling and rising up like a cobra. Smooth and white, it resembled something dead, like a maggot that writhed in rotten meat.

In an instant, the room dissolved, and revealed what lay beneath; the fallen remnants of a stone hall with high walls, where bones lay piled on the ground, black and mouldering. The creature was a sea-serpent, but its snaky form was another deception, like the beautiful woman or the white, skull-faced monarch from the deep. Though its power lay in its ability to cause fear, they were in real danger; Yuste had been right to say that it lived off blood in the water – and carrion, the rotting remains of its victims, scattered underfoot.

The serpent hissed, but they had one advantage; Cricri had taken it by surprise. Hand in hand, the children ran for the door, which was now a broken archway in one wall. One by one, they dived through, and Aude was the last to go, pushing Cricri in front of her. She could not help glancing back, and saw the snake's face as it barrelled towards her, opening a red mouth that gaped into a deep, intestinal tube, as if a string of entrails had come to life.

Aude choked. She had looked into its eyes, and it had seen her; she knew it had marked her in some way, marked her for death, as if there could be no escape from that gaping maw. Then Cricri seized her wrist and dragged her through the door, and she was in the sea, struggling as he pulled her after him, up through the water.

Aude had no breath left in her lungs. Her head pulsed, and she thought her skull would explode. If it had not been for Cricri, she would have drowned; but he kept beside her, and the force of his kicking swept them upwards, through water that seemed dark and all-enfolding.

In the silence, she could make out a wallowing sound, and she knew the sea-serpent was following them. It would move fast in the water; it could catch them and swallow them like minnows.

Her head broke the surface, and she howled. Someone was reaching out to catch hold of her, and Aude fought him, until she realised it was Gustave. He hauled her into the boat, while the others scrambled over the side, making the small craft rock alarmingly.

'Quick!' shouted Yuda. 'We have to go...'

The snake's head broke the surface, and carried on rising out of the sea, smooth and slick, until it towered high as a chimney above them. Its grey body glimmered with mucus, and its eyes were the colour of fire.

'By the Mother!' said Gustave, sitting down heavily in the boat and making it wallow. He snatched up an oar to use as a weapon, and the Vasilyevich twins, unsteady on their feet, arm in arm, pointed their hands up at the serpent's head as it descended, its black tongue flickering in and out. Aude and Cricri fought to steady the boat, while Francois sat with his hand on the tiller. Without anyone to row, they were stuck, and the snake was too quick for them to outpace it.

Gustave brandished the oar over his head, and the twins fired together, with blue and silver flame; Aude noticed how much brighter it was than the time she had seen them first. She felt an odd sensation at her midriff, as if her heart had skipped a beat; Yuste was accurate, and Yuda was strong. Together they made a perfect team, but she wondered whether they would ever be content with that.

The flame stung the snake, and it flinched aside, whipping its huge neck round in a coil. Gustave sat down hard and struggled to fit his oar into the rowlock, before beginning to row with all his strength. Cricri snatched up the second pair of oars and did the same. The twins stayed on their feet, watching for the snake's return.

Aude staggered over to them and crouched down in the bottom of the boat. She could hear the slap of the oars in the water and the frightened breathing of the other children.

'It wants me,' she said. 'If I jump into the water and let it take me, you will get away.'

The twins looked down at her in astonishment.

'Don't you dare!' shouted Yuste. 'That would be a wicked thing to do. You've done nothing wrong.'

'It won't be satisfied,' said Yuda, wiping his nose on his wet sleeve. 'It wants us all.'

Aude did not ask him how he knew, but she stayed where she was, though she felt drawn to the water, the dark water, that called out to her. Then Yuste stooped and touched her, and she felt as if her eyes filled with light; sunlight, the morning and the rush of cool air from the approaching dawn.

'Stay with us, Aude,' said Yuste.

Aude blinked. She was in the boat, in the dark, with Gustave and Cricri rowing for their lives, and François holding the tiller steady. Behind them she could see the snake gliding through the waves like the prow of a Northman's ship, the ones in the stories.

'Will it follow us for ever?' she said in a whisper.

'I don't know,' said Yuda. He and Yuste, arms round each other, turned to face the snake. Aude would have liked to stand up too, but she feared losing her balance or making the boat capsize. She was not surprised when the twins sat down together; they leaned over the stern, watching the sea-serpent as it swam after them; it was gaining on them.

'Can't you go any faster?' said Yuda over his shoulder. Gustave and Cricri swore at him.

'We're still a long way from the shore,' said Yuste. 'It'll catch us before we get there.'

Aude caught at his sleeve, and he gave her a worried look. 'I've got an idea,' she said. 'If it is after me... perhaps we can trick it...'

She whispered her idea, and the twins agreed with great reluctance. They moved to let Aude sit in the stern, and she leaned out over the edge as far as she dared, stretching out her arms towards the snake as if she were calling to it. She could sense that it knew her, that its mind was focussed on her more than the others. It saw her as a wounded bird, something easy to catch and devour. Her song, and her sadness, had taught it that.

Aude shut her eyes. It was better not to see; but even with her eyes closed she recalled the emptiness in the hollow sockets that had fixed on her. When she was dead, her head would become an empty skull with blank eyes; death had infected her, reaching inside to twist her with coldness. The price she paid, and the price she would pay; there was no escape from this, even if the sea failed to claim her tonight.

Magic always had a price; any magic, even something like the powers the twins had been born with. They had not learned that yet – or Yuste had not; Yuda had discovered it too soon, when he defended himself against Olivier Baudoin.

'Aude, it's coming,' whispered Yuste.

Aude forced herself to open her eyes. The snake seemed close. She felt she had caught its attention; it was bearing down on the small boat, getting ready to stoop and snatch her up. She was the bait, and she must stay calm until the last minute.

When the snake was almost on top of the boat, it reared up again, its neck soaring out of the water, smooth as a worm, and she saw the long, muscular ridges of its body break the surface. Her heart pounded, and she felt as if it were beating against her ribs. She looked up into the face, little more than a lozenge of jaws and eyes; and she felt it staring at her, how tiny she was, and choice, a morsel.

Aude whispered a prayer. In spite of herself, the words of a Doxan prayer came into her mouth. *Please, Holy Mother, don't let it take me. Not this time. I will light a candle to you in the church. I will be a good daughter of Doxa if you spare us.*

The snake rose high above her, and she knew it was ready to strike, but the speed with which it moved still surprised her. The mouth gaped, and the tongue reached towards her. It stooped so fast she felt she would be swallowed up, engulfed by the red tunnel of its throat, before she had time to cry out.

The twins did as she had asked. As the snake opened its mouth, dislocating its jaw to swallow her, they sprang to their feet and fired, together, straight into the throat. Aude saw the two jets of fire spiralling upwards, and heard the rush of flame and a roar like thunder that seemed to split her head open.

The lightning seared the snake's gullet and sent it flailing backwards, writhing and shuddering as if it had been struck by lightning. It gave a horrible, tearing scream that Aude heard as a thin shriek, deafened as she was by the sound of shaman-fire. She clung to the side of the boat, with Yuste and Yuda beside her, and watched the sea-serpent vanishing beneath the waves, and the hissing noise as the water quenched the fire in its throat. Both twins put an arm round her at once, and she felt their heat, even though they were soaking wet. They felt as hot to the touch as two loaves of bread fresh from the oven.

The thought made Aude smile. She wished she knew what it felt like to have such powers, even if there was a price. She could feel their exhilaration just by being close to them. They had not destroyed the serpent, but they had driven it away, back to its lair, for who knows how many years?

'Do you think we killed it?' said Yuste.

'I don't think it was alive in the first place,' said Yuda. He shivered, as if unaware of the heat coming from his skin.

'It won't forget us,' said Aude.

'That doesn't matter,' he said. 'Nothing bad can happen to you as long as we're still here.'

***

When they rowed in to the shore, they were surprised to find a group of adults waiting for them on the beach, with lanterns in their hands. As soon as Aude had climbed out of the boat, she saw that Doctor and Madame Vasilyevich were there, with Prakhash Sival, her mother and Thibault, Cricri's mother, Francois's father and Gustave's parents.

They were seized by their respective families, wrapped in blankets and scolded. Aude guessed that Thibault had raised the alarm, and was glad. She managed to snatch a secret smile at him, and saw him turn red with guilt and relief. Trying to ignore her mother, though she was glad of the warm blanket, she kept turning round to see if she could see what had happened to the others, particularly the twins. She was curious about Doctor Vasilyevich, because she had only glimpsed him before; a tall man in a black frock coat, wearing a beaver hat shaped like a drum, perched on top his head. His black beard streaked was with grey, and he wore gold pince-nez perched on his nose.

The Vasilyevich family seemed to be scolding the twins more quietly than everyone else. Perhaps it had come of the habit of not wanting to draw too much attention to themselves. But Prakhash Sival noticed Aude looking round, smiled and came to speak to her.

'Madame,' he said, bowing to Aude's mother, who smiled in return.

'We dived on Savorin! We only just escaped,' said Aude, excitedly. Her mother sighed.

Sival said, 'The twins said something to that effect. It's hard to make out what they mean. They are babbling about a sea-serpent.'

Aude felt reluctant to say anything about what they had experienced. She wondered how much of it they could tell their parents.

'Maybe,' she said, looking away. 'Something attacked us. The twins drove it off.'

Sival laid his hand on her shoulder, and smiled into her eyes. 'You're tired, Aude,' he said. 'It will be better tomorrow. You can tell us all about it after you've had a rest.'

***

She did not tell them about it that day, or the next. Instead, something changed. Everyone in the village, even her father and older brothers, treated them with more respect. No-one said anything, but she noticed that the farmers, the shopkeepers and even the fishermen tipped their hats or acknowledged the children whenever they met. Not just her or her brother, but all the others – Cricri the bastard, François the lame, Gustave the fat, and the Wanderer twins who were also shamans.

Perhaps the people of Sankt Eglis knew more about Savorin than they let on. And perhaps a ghost had been laid, for the time being. Aude felt less like a child than she had done when she first came to the village and met the twins. She could not imagine swimming naked in the sea, happy and careless, as she had done before. Her body began to change, and she found herself spending more time with Yuste and the girls of her age; the boys in their class were less interesting.

Perhaps for that reason, the gang broke up. One of the fishermen took Cricri as his apprentice. François' father acknowledged his son's intelligence, and sent him away to study at the technical school in Masalyar. Gustave grew stronger and less stout, and went to work on his family's farm. The only ones left at school were Aude and the twins, and they were kept busy by their families. Yuda had to study the Law of the Wanderers with his father, practice the vyel and work with Sival; Yuste had much the same, though since she was not studying the Law her mother had much to teach her about keeping a Clean home.

Aude herself was expected to help on the farm, work with her mother in the still room making preserves, pickles and medicines, and learn the important skills of spinning, weaving and dress-making that were highly prized by the Women, and passed down from mother to daughter. They were not merely about making a dowry, or showing that you would be an obedient and useful wife; Aelis explained that these skills enabled you to run your own household, whether you were married, single or a widow.

When Aude next met the twins, they were all wearing adult clothes. Yuste and Yuda were dressed head to foot in black, apart from their white shirts. Yuda wore a big hat with a wide brim, and a skull-cap underneath. On hot days, he was permitted to take off his coat and work in his shirt-sleeves, but he had to wear a four-cornered garment like a prayer-shawl under his shirt, with four fringes. Yuste had to dress modestly, which meant covering her legs. Aude too had to wear a full-length skirt.

They met on the beach, feeling like awkward little puppets.

'I hate all this,' said Aude, shaking her skirt.

The twins nodded. They both seemed overwhelmed by their clothes, as if they had been taken captive by serge and starched linen.

'We never have any time to play or do anything fun,' said Yuste.

Yuda nudged her. His face cracked open into a huge smile. 'Nobody can see us here,' he said. 'The only person who comes here is Sival.'

The three of them looked at each other and started to laugh. Then they pulled off their hated outer clothes and threw them in a heap, one after the other. The girls kept on their chemises and petticoats, and Yuda his shirt and drawers. They laughed at each other's appearance; they were all bony and thin, and neither Yuste nor Aude had developed much in the way of breasts, though both girls folded their arms. But they were free again, released from the carapace of adulthood that had been imposed on them from outside.

'Race you!' shouted Yuda and set off at a run, with the girls after him, laughing and shouting that he was cheating. They were free and safe, with nothing to trouble them.

And deep down, beneath the dark waters of the bay, the sea-serpent of Savorin lay in dreamless sleep. Waiting for the next time, waiting for blood in the water.

THE END

Also by Jessica Rydill

The *Mir: Shamansworld* series published by Kristell Ink and available from Amazon

Children of the Shaman

Young Annat is doubly cursed: an outcast Wanderer and a Shaman, born with uncanny powers. She has no wish to meet the father she never knew. But Yuda is also a powerful Shaman, whose powers can heal - and kill. When Annat's brother vanishes, she must go with Yuda into a perilous underworld, where she will learn how to use magic - if she survives.

The Glass Mountain

As crows return to the skies over Masalyar, dark magic is at work.

When Annat's brother vanishes from his university, the young shaman and her aunt Yuste set out to find him. But soon they learn that Malchik is not the only one in danger; a Magus from Sklava wants to raise an old enemy from the dead, and for that he needs both Malchik and Annat's souls, and the heart of their father, thrice-powerful shaman Yuda Vasilyevich.

With Annat and Malchik captive in the Glass Mountain, an army under the Doyen of Ademar marching on their homeland and a trap laid for Yuda, Yuste may be the only one who can save her family – and her country. But Yuste lost her powers years ago; and her only allies are a burned-out shaman-detective, an old warrior, and the Doyen's youngest son.

In the forests of the North, Yuste must confront her true self, her twin brother – and the wolves.

Malarat

The Duc de Malarat wants to conquer the Kingdom of Lefranu. In his army ride the ruthless and fanatical Domini Canes, warrior monks of the Inquisition who have forged a secret weapon to cripple the power of the shamans.

But when Malarat's eldest son challenges a stranger to a duel, he sets in motion a terrifying train of events. For the stranger is Malchik Vasilyevich, now a man; and his sister Annat stands with her allies and the Railway People as a fully-trained shaman, prepared to defend the city of Yonar from Malarat's army.

But Malchik and Annat will face foes much worse than the Duc de Malarat, even as the struggle that began in Lefranu spreads to the spirit world and beyond.

Winterbloom

Sophie Vasilyevich is a teenager growing up in Anglond, the child of exiles. Sometimes grass springs up where she walks, and her future holds an unusual fate: she is going to be kidnapped when she is sixteen, and no one can stop it.

Taken between worlds to the city of Bath in 1920s England, Sophie meets a young man called James Carnwallis, once a pilot in the Great War. But even as she falls in love, she learns more about the forces at work – and her fate in their plans.

As an alliance of shamans, ghosts and gods assembles in a desperate attempt to recover Sophie and prevent the destruction of their worlds, they find that their only hope may lie in Sophie's gift, and in the Greenwood: a power older than time itself.

About the author

Jessica Rydill is a British fantasy author from the West Country. She was born in 1959. She studied at King's College, Cambridge and the College of Law, working as a solicitor for 13 years. Her travels in Israel, France, Eastern Europe and Southern Africa have provided some of the inspiration for her writing.

Her first novel, *Children of the Shaman,* was published by Orbit in 2001, and short-listed for the Locus magazine best first novel in 2002. A sequel, *The Glass Mountain*, appeared in October 2002. Both books have been reissued by small press Kristell Ink, together with sequels *Malarat* and *Winterbloom*.

Jessica lives near Bath with her husband and her collection of ball-jointed dolls , which really aren't creepy. Though they can be badly behaved...

Visit Jessica's web-site at www.shamansland.com
to learn more about Mir, the shamanworld.
Sign up to her mailing list at:
https://mailchi.mp/06e15605103b/shamanslandnews

Printed in Poland
by Amazon Fulfillment
Poland Sp. z o.o., Wrocław

Printed in Poland
by Amazon Fulfillment
Poland Sp. z o.o., Wrocław

51546614R00051